MICHELLE **PFEIFFER**

GEORGE **CLOONEY**

ONE FINE DAY

TWENTIETH CENTURY FOX PRESENTS A LYNDA OBST PRODUCTION IN ASSOCIATION WITH VIA ROSA PRODUCTIONS A MICHAEL HOFFMAN FILM MICHELLE PFEIFFER GEORGE CLOONEY "ONE FINE DAY" MAE WHITMAN and CHARLES DURNING MUSIC BY JAMES NEWTON HOWARD FILM EDITOR GARTH CRAVEN AND MICHE... PRODUCTION DESIGNER DAVID GROPMAN DIRECTOR OF PHOTOGRAPHY OLIVER STAPLETON CO-PRODUCER MARY McLAGLEN EXECUTIVE PRODUCERS KATE GUINZBURG AND MICHE... WRITTEN BY TERREL SELTZER AND ELLEN SIMON PRODUCED BY LYNDA OBST DIRECTED BY MICHAEL HOFFMAN

READ THE NOVEL BY ST. MARTIN'S PAPERBACKS   SOUNDTRACK AVAILABLE ON COLUMBIA CDs & CASSETTES

PG PARENTAL GUIDANCE SUGGESTED
SOME MATERIAL MAY NOT BE SUITABLE FOR CHILDREN

DOLBY
SELECTED THEATRES

ONE FINE DAY

A novel by H.B. Gilmour
Based on a screenplay by
Terrel Seltzer and Ellen Simon

St. Martin's Paperbacks

NOTE: If you purchased this book without a cover you should be aware that this book is stolen property. It was reported as "unsold and destroyed" to the publisher, and neither the author nor the publisher has received any payment for this "stripped book."

ONE FINE DAY

Copyright © 1997 by Twentieth Century Fox Film Corporation. All rights reserved.

Cover photograph copyright © 1997 by Twentieth Century Fox Film Corporation. All rights reserved.

All rights reserved. No part of this book may be used or reproduced in any manner whatsoever without written permission except in the case of brief quotations embodied in critical articles or reviews. For information address St. Martin's Press, 175 Fifth Avenue, New York, NY 10010.

ISBN: 0-312-96115-4

Printed in the United States of America

St. Martin's Paperbacks edition/January 1997

St. Martin's Paperbacks are published by St. Martin's Press, 175 Fifth Avenue, New York, NY 10010.

10 9 8 7 6 5 4 3 2 1

— Prologue —

In a flowing gown and flawless hairdo, Snow White warbled a tune about the prince who was to come to rescue her.

In torn jeans and a faded sweatshirt, Melanie Parker plucked a pair of jockey shorts out of her laundry basket and, folding them, absently hummed along to the *Snow White* song coming off the VCR in the background. The shorts, bright red with superheroes on the fly, belonged to Sammy who, at the moment, lay sprawled across Mel's bed oblivious to Snow White's dreams and desires.

A soft spring rain pattered against her bedroom window. Sammy had fallen asleep about five minutes into the video. A few hours earlier, he'd shaken his head when Mel pulled the cassette out of her leather tote bag. "Mom," he'd gasped in disbelief, "that's for girls."

"Well, I'm a girl," Mel had reminded him. "And I used to like this movie." She hadn't added, I used to believe in the tooth fairy, too. No, seeing Sammy stiffen at the irritable edge in her voice, she'd caught herself. On the enamel-top table she'd rescued from a Second Avenue junk shop, Mel had set down the cassette, the grocery bags, her keys, her giant leather shoulder bag, and the crayon drawing Sammy had lovingly presented to her when she'd picked him up at Eastside Montessori's afterschool program.

"I'm sorry, honey," she'd said, kneeling so their eyes met—Mel's yellow-green as a cat's, Sammy's blue-green and inconceivably innocent. "They didn't have Mighty Morphins at the video store. It was out. And I thought you might like this one. It's pretty scary," she'd added hopefully.

Pretty scary was right. Here she was mindlessly humming the twentieth century's most subversive theme song. Be a patient, pretty, good little girl, and gullible, too, it urged—and someday your very own prince will show up to save you.

At least it had put Sammy to sleep, Mel thought now. She tossed the folded red shorts onto the pile at the foot of her bed and, in the flickering blue light of the TV screen, studied the remarkable sweet face of her six-year-old son.

As if he could feel her eyes on him, Sammy stirred. His dark lashes fluttered, his cherubic lips released a small sigh. A tangle of curls lay mashed against his soft cheeks—which reminded Mel that he needed a haircut. She added this information to the To-Do list she kept on the night table beside her bed. Then, blowing her own unruly sun-streaked hair out of her eyes, she glanced again at Sammy's angelic face. This time she noticed a dark stain on his nostrils.

A nose bleed, Mel thought, frightened suddenly. The stain was sticky to the touch. She sniffed, she tasted, she laughed with relief. "Ice cream," she murmured. Then she clamped her hand over her mouth to keep from blurting out, "Oh no, the ice cream!"

On the kitchen counter, in a gradually expanding chocolate puddle, sat the half-gallon of frozen ice cream Mel had opened an hour ago. Also on the counter, two bags of partially unpacked groceries rebuked her. In one of them was the fresh ground peanut butter she'd picked up at Health Nuts to make Sammy's lunch for tomorrow. As she put away the groceries, she smiled, remembering how excited Sammy was about the field trip.

"We're going on the Circle Line, Mom," he'd enthused on their way home from school. "All around New York. On a real boat, Mom."

If it stopped raining, Mel caught herself thinking.

The automatic pessimism brought her up short. When had this happened? she wondered. She turned on the tap water, soaked and wrung out a sponge, and began to mop up the melting ice cream. Where was that warbling optimism she'd had when she was Snow White's age?

That bright determination and boundless energy had made her believe she could juggle school, marriage, motherhood, and a career as easily as the street performers outside the Metropolitan Museum kept six, eight, ten balls in the air. That manic optimism had seen her through Pratt and her architecture degree. It had also convinced her that marrying Eddie Parker, a musician as handsome as Sting, as hedonistic as Jagger, and as practical as Peter Pan, was a great idea.

When the balls started falling, he was the first to go.

Mel put the soggy lid back on the Eddys No Fat Vanilla Fudge and carried the container to the refrigerator. The freezer door was propped open by mounds of ice. Inside, microwavable frozen dinners were sweating with the effort of staying cold.

Defrost fridge, Mel scrawled on her kitchen list. Was it really two years ago? She paused with the pencil still in her hand. Could it be two years since Eddie had left the apartment with his practice pad and drumsticks in one hand, a duffle bag in the other and, hanging from his head, the satin Bon Jovi tour jacket she'd hurled at him?

"Mel, be reasonable," he'd urged. "It was a road thing. I don't even remember her name." They were standing in the foyer—the foyer she'd sponge-painted when she was pregnant with Sammy, while Eddie was in a studio on 54th Street each night until dawn, offering moral support to another drummer whose debut album was being cut.

"Whisper," she'd reminded him. "When she called, she said her name was Whisper."

"Come on, Mel. That's not a real name. Whisper?

You can't end a marriage because of someone named Whisper. I mean, how can you take that seriously?"

"It's not about her, it's us," Mel had tried again to explain. "It's how you're never here, for Sammy, for me . . . How your word means nothing. Your promises mean nothing. I mean, look at you, Eddie, you can't even show up for some poor little groupie from South Jersey who says you promised her Foo Fighter tickets."

He'd turned red then. He was outraged, even worse, embarrassed. "Okay," he'd said. "Okay. Okay. You think I promised her concert tickets, okay."

"Don't you get it?" Mel had shouted. "It's not about tickets or groupies or your being on the road. It's about you being pathologically absent. Even when you're here."

"You know why, Mel? You know why?" he'd challenged her. "Because you don't *need* me here, that's why. Because you're so damn together you don't need anyone or anything. And if you did, you'd just add it to one of your goddamn lists—and pick it up on the way home from work!"

"That's not true," she'd countered lamely, "that is so unfair." And then, stung, heartsick, unable to make him understand, she'd begun to cry. And here she was now, still making lists. Mel laughed and put the pencil down next to the pad on the counter.

She had wanted to hold onto her anger, she remembered. She'd wanted to stay mad at Eddie, for

Sammy's sake if not for her own. She'd wanted to blame him for . . . what? For being who he was and had always been? For being the exact same Eddie Parker she'd married and had her beautiful baby with?

Eddie hadn't changed. She had.

And, panicked, he'd rushed out the door. At least that's what he claimed his shrink had told him. That her sudden vulnerability, those unexpected tears, had frightened him. He'd panicked because he'd realized she *did* need something, and he didn't have it to give.

So he ran.

He hadn't even waited for the elevator.

What had seemed heartbreaking then seemed comic to her now. The sound of Eddie's rubber soles bounding down the hall stairs. Like a juggler's dropped ball bouncing away, Mel thought suddenly. That's what it had sounded like. That's what it was.

She was tired, probably punchy, she decided. She went into her bedroom and gently shook Sammy awake. It was nearly ten o'clock. "Time to get into your own bed, sweetie," she whispered, helping him to his feet and leading him down the short hallway to his room.

"Don't forget to feed the fish, Mom," Sammy mumbled as she tucked him in.

"I fed them before, sweetie. They're fine." Sammy had been given the honor of keeping the class fish this week. There were three of them, a flowing gold one, a skinny black one, and a red and white one with a mean face. All three, Mel was relieved to note, were still circling the bowl. Not a belly-up disaster in seven days. Tomorrow it was some other lucky family's turn. The fish were due back at school in the morning.

" 'Night, sweetie." She kissed Sammy's cheek and headed for the door.

"Mommy . . . Mom," he called. "What happened to that girl?"

"What girl, honey? Were you having a dream?"

"No, you know, the one who was singing with the birds."

"Oh, that girl. Snow White. A prince came. She lived happily ever after," Mel assured him.

She hurried back to the kitchen, finished the dinner dishes, made Sammy's lunch, packed his soccer gear, and Vitamin C because he'd sneezed a couple of times during supper, and, yes, rainwear, just in case. Then she placed the Power Rangers' Lunch Box next to Sammy's backpack and her own black leather bag on the kitchen table, and went into the bathroom to brush her teeth.

She brushed, she gargled, she fished Sammy's soggy toys out of the bathtub and checked her hand washables to see if they were drying. And then she caught sight of herself in the full length mirror on the bathroom door.

It was an old mirror, and kind. Its reflections were soft and blurry, and it had a tendency to round one's edges voluptuously. Mel needed such a friend tonight. She needed not to see the fatigue lines etched in her face, the dark hollows under her eyes, the first thin necklace of age circling her pale throat.

She stretched her neck and stuck out her tongue, a face-toning exercise her mother had recently recommended. Then she gave up and laughed. She guessed she was still attractive. Construction workers, delivery men, and bicycle messengers were generally enthusiastic about her. Not that they were connoisseurs, of course. Not a choosy bunch, she realized. Still, some of them were young and good-looking and seemed surprisingly sincere.

She knew she had great legs, and slim, muscular arms. Her father's legacy. He'd been trim and athletic to the end. She looked well in clothes. Her sister Liza, a black belt consumer who had married into a Fifth Avenue co-op and a Bergdorf's Gold Card, accused her of staying thin just to avoid shopping. It was probably true. She hated shlepping through crowded department stores and minimalist boutiques. She didn't keep up with trends. She'd always been more interested in the detail and construction of clothing than style.

As if to prove it, Mel slipped into her favorite nightie, an oversized pin-striped Brooks Brothers shirt from the Eddie era. She'd found it in a San Francisco thrift shop when Eddie was playing a gig out there. He'd asked her to come with him. It must have been pretty early in their courtship.

Buttoning the soft cotton shirt, Mel went down the

hall to her bedroom, where she rewound and turned off the video, cleared Sammy's toys and story books off her bed, and decided to take one last look at the work she'd brought home: architectural diagrams and report sheets on the proposed Yates & Yates shopping center.

Big day tomorrow. Big presentation. Oh yes, and she had to take Sammy's friend Maggie to school tomorrow morning. Mel willed herself to remember. Then got up and trudged back to the kitchen and left a big note next to Sammy's lunch box: *Pick up Maggie*.

Maggie's mother, Kristin, from 12C, had landed her Prince Charming. Dr. Charming, actually. Gregg Spizer was responsible, stable, kind . . . even attractive, in a 52-year-old orthodontist sort of way. Bless them both, Mel thought. After the ex from hell, Kristin deserved a good, dependable grownup. From what she'd heard, Maggie's father was another no-show charmer who dragged his six-year-old daughter to Knicks or Rangers games once a month after a dinner of Papaya King hot dogs and Dove bars.

The clock on the night table said eleven-forty-five. Mel flipped through the diagrams, then put them aside and turned off the light. She snuggled beneath the cotton quilt and was just falling asleep when she remembered. Pulling herself out of bed, Mel shuffled down the hall and double-locked the front door. Impulsively, she peered through the peephole. The hallway was empty. Not a prince in sight.

— One —

New York is never still. Not even its rivers are allowed to rest.

A tug boat chugged through the swirling dark waters of the East River, leaving a wake of foam and rolling waves. Rain pocked the river's surface, dappling the gaudy reflections of traffic along FDR Drive and over the bridges mooring the island. While the club scene kicked into gear downtown, the upper east side hit the sack early during the week. By midnight, the few rumpled drunks still in their business suits hailed cabs along Third Avenue and headed home. The whoosh of taxis streaking through the rain, the distant lament of the tug boat's horn, the laugh track from the television set next door, all provided an irresistible lullaby. Melanie slept.

"Mommy . . . Mom!"

Her eyes popped open. Sammy's face, inches from

her own, came into focus. He was wide awake.

"I'm really thirsty, Mommy," he said.

"No," Mel mumbled. "You're not."

"Yeah. Really," he insisted. "I really am, Mommy."

Mel sent him back to his room, shuffled half-asleep into the kitchen and filled a glass with tap water for him. In the glow of his nightlight, she handed Sammy the glass and tried not to glare as he drank it very slowly. Finally, Mel took the nearly empty glass from his hands. "Okay, goodnight," she said, kissing his head.

"Wait!" Sammy commanded. "There's one more sip left."

"It's only half a sip," Mel argued on her way out of the room. "You don't need it. Goodnight."

"I do need it. I do need it, Mommy," he called plaintively.

She returned and gave him the glass, then whisked it away the instant he'd swallowed the last sip. "Okay, now goodnight for real," she said, and kissed him again.

" 'Night, Mommy." Sammy slid down and pulled the covers up to his chin. "I'm really excited to go on the trip tomorrow, Mom. I love big boats."

"That's good," Mel said, stooping to retrieve George, Sammy's stuffed monkey. She adjusted George's red cap, then propped him back up on the bookshelf.

"The Circle Line is big, right?"

"Yup," Mel said, closing the window against the

rain, which was coming down harder now.

"Mom?" Sammy called, as she was halfway to the door.

"Shhh. Sleepy time now."

"Is Daddy coming to my soccer game tomorrow?"

Mel stopped with her hand on the doorknob. Okay, it was time to walk that fine line again. Tread gently between truth and hope, she warned herself, and try not to trample either one.

"He's going to try, Sammy," she said gently. Then she returned to his bed and sat down next to him. "Remember I explained to you that Daddy has a . . . a different schedule than a lot of other daddies?"

"Yeah," Sammy said, waiting, wanting more.

Mel smoothed back the warm curls stuck to his forehead and cheeks. "Well, musicians don't always know exactly when and where they'll play, or even who they'll get a chance to play with, you know? So he might not be able to come tomorrow."

"But he's gonna try, right?" Sammy urged.

"Yes he will." Mel hugged him. He was so little, but sturdy, she marvelled. She could feel his skinny shoulder blades through his Power Rangers pajamas. They were delicate as birds' wings. Yet his arms around her neck were wiry with promise. "I love you a million, billion, zillion," she said.

"Do you love him?" Sammy asked.

"Your Daddy?" Mel closed her eyes and snuggled her face against Sammy's sleek damp hair. No, was the answer, not any more, not for a while now. When

Eddie appeared as promised, when he showed up for their son, she was flooded with relief, gratitude. Those were the emotions that had replaced love, she guessed. Of course, Sammy's beautiful blue-green eyes and dark lashes, his little shoulders and curly hair . . . she loved them . . . and they were Eddie's.

"I love your Daddy," she murmured into Sammy's ear, "because he gave me you. Now go to sleep."

She pulled up his covers and smoothed his curls once more. His eyes were closed, his breathing easy and even at last. He was asleep. She tiptoed to the door. "Please let Eddie come, please let Eddie come," she whispered in the dark.

Back in her room, Mel settled gratefully into bed and closed her eyes. When she opened them, it was twelve after twelve, and Sammy was staring at her.

"I can't sleep, Mom. I had a bad dream," he announced.

"In just two minutes you already fell asleep and had a bad dream?"

Sammy nodded earnestly. "I'm really scared," he said.

Mel propped herself up on one elbow. "Okay, what did you dream?"

Sammy shrugged. "I don't remember. But no kidding, it was scary."

"No kidding. Well . . ." Mel sat up. "I checked for monsters under your bed, and there weren't any. So there's nothing to be scared—"

A deafening crack of lightning turned the bedroom bright as day. Sammy jumped into Mel's instantly outstretched arm. Rattled as the leaves against the sheeting rain outside, they clung to one another.

"Please, Mom, can I—" Sammy said at last.

"Absolutely," said Mel, turning back the bedcovers. "Come on. Get in."

At three-fifteen a.m., Mel gasped and grabbed her eye. Someone had assaulted her while she slept. Struggling up through layers of exhaustion, she hauled herself to a sitting position. In the darkened bedroom, she listened to the tattoo of rain on the window panes, and gingerly tested her eye. She could blink, but it was painful.

Beside her, Sammy was sound asleep. His arms and legs were outstretched, splayed as if he were measuring the bed. Mel stared at him suspiciously, then lifted one of his small coiled fists. The one nearest to her. The one that, she was now convinced, had just punched her in the eye. Was it possible? Such a small fist? Such a big hurt?

She groped for her night table list and, in the dark, somewhere under *Sammy haircut* she hoped, scrawled *Excedrin*. Then she pushed the pad away, dislodging the sheaf of shopping-center diagrams which fluttered to the floor. Leave them, Mel admonished herself. Go back to sleep.

Instead, she quietly slid open the night table drawer and found her emergency flashlight. Then, easing herself out of bed, she gathered up the fallen diagrams. As long as she was awake, she guessed maybe she should go over the figures again. Why not, she had one good eye left.

The alarm went off at six-thirty. Mel reached for the clock and felt the shopping-center plans crumple under her rib cage. She pushed down the snooze alarm and rolled onto her back. The flashlight tumbled off the bed and hit the floor. Its plastic head popped off. Its miniature bulb skittered under the night table. With a terrible clatter, batteries bounced and rolled across the floor.

Sammy turned suddenly in his sleep, arms flailing. Instinctively, Mel ducked and covered her injured eye. The pain had pretty much passed. A gentle fingertip exam proved that there wasn't much swelling. A minor shiner, Mel reckoned. Nothing makeup wouldn't hide. Well, that was good news, a momentous beginning to another fine day. Melanie Parker rolled over and went back to sleep.

6:30 A.M.

A plump gray pigeon plunged off Melanie's window ledge and soared west toward Central Park. In the thin morning mist, the pigeon lady waited, her black handbag stuffed with bread-crumbs, rice, and crackers. Joggers in spandex and sweats pounded around the reservoir's cinder track, splashing through shallow puddles left by last night's downpour. And on Central Park West, the pothole repair crew reviewed its options for visiting chaos on the upper west side of the city. Trapping motorists in a single bus-fume–befouled lane, then assaulting them with a range of ear-shattering, mind-numbing noises was the most obvious choice.

A moment before Jack Taylor's alarm clock went off, a worker in a hardhat and bright yellow plastic overalls wedged a jackhammer against his girdled gut and, shouting "Good morning, New York!" turned on the juice.

Jack Taylor woke groaning. Spread-eagle, stretched out parallel to the headboard of his king-size bed, he groped blindly for the beeping alarm clock. A punishing pounding filled his head. With one eye, Jack focused in on the bottle of Excedrin beside the clock. No contest. His hand forgot the alarm and seized the Excedrin.

What had he done to deserve this? Now there was a familiar question, Jack mused, struggling with the childproof cap. He was wearing his boxer shorts, he noticed. Okay, no story there. But a glance toe-ward confirmed a discomforting suspicion: he'd fallen asleep in his shoes. Not a good sign.

Nor was the interminable banging noise. He tried again to yank open the Excedrin bottle and it flew from his hands, rolling off the bed. No big deal, Jack reasoned. It wouldn't have warded off the stroke he was having.

Had he been with a woman last night? Closed an after hours club? Chased a drug bust story into Alphabet City, or an exposé on pit bull fighting through the projects? Had he stopped in at a sports bar and left with the resident linebacker's date when the big guy went off to relieve himself? In other words, had he made a fool of himself doing any of the hundred and one remorse-provoking things he routinely did?

No, Jack decided. He ran his fingers through his hair, clamping his pounding head. The way he remembered it, he was practically a monk these days. He hadn't been with a woman in months. He hadn't, in fact, had a minute to screw up since he'd broken the mayor's kickback story.

That was it. He'd been out in Queens, at Manny Feldstein's sister's fiftieth birthday party. He'd been stuck out there half the night, in a catering hall, drinking sweet red wine and doing the Hora with Manny's Aunt Ida, and the Hully-Gully with his nieces Dawn and Sabra, one of whom wanted to be a writer.

But Jack owed Manny. Owed him big. Manny Feldstein had given him the dirt on His Honor, Mayor Aikens. Manny Feldstein had risked his chubby little neck to give Jack the biggest story of his career.

A muffled voice cut through the banging. A familiar voice. "Jack, please, please, please be there."

Someone was banging on his front door. And there

was a jackhammer tearing up the street. And his alarm clock was beeping.

Jack jumped out of bed and hurried to the door. Rushing through the disaster zone formerly known as his living room, he barely glanced at the scaffolding. They'd been working on the broken ceiling pipe for weeks.

"Jack, are you there? Please?"

Kristin? What was his ex-wife doing pounding on his door at six-thirty in the morning? He opened the door and caught her mid-knock.

"Er, hi, Jack," she said, apologetically.

"Hi," he responded, then noticed she was staring at his shoes. He shook his head. "Your guess is as good as mine," he said, just as his six-year-old daughter emerged from behind her mother and shouted, "Boo!"

"Maggie Magpie!" Jack knelt down and caught her in his arms. "Boo to you, Miss Maggie Sue. How's my best girl?"

"She's staying with you for the rest of the week?" Kristin said hopefully.

Jack straightened up. "Excuse me?" he said, with Maggie in his arms. "What are you talking about?"

"Put me down, put me down, Daddy. I want to play on the jungle gym."

Jack released his energetic little daughter and she ran directly to the tall, elaborate scaffolding set up around the exposed pipes, and began to climb up on it.

"Maggie, be careful!" Kristin cautioned. "I can't believe you still haven't gotten your plumbing fixed, Jack."

"I do it all the time, Mommy," Maggie called.

"She's fine," he said, waiting.

"What's that noise, Daddy?"

"What noise?" he asked. "Kristin, what's going on here?"

His ex-wife looked alarmingly like the hapless stewardess she'd once been, all blue-eyed and blonde and dressed for traveling. Now she said in her best pointing-out-the-safety-features-of-the-craft voice, "It's Daddy's alarm clock, Maggie. Why don't you go see if you can find it?"

"Okay, Mommy!" Jack's exquisite daughter climbed off the scaffolding and headed for his bedroom.

"And then turn it off," Kristin called after her.

Jack took the opportunity to grab his raincoat off the hall rack. He slipped into it, tied the belt, and waited for Kristin's explanation.

The minute Maggie was out of earshot, she said, "Well, you know that Gregg and I got married last Saturday . . ."

"Right. Congratulations again. How is Gregg?"

"He's downstairs, waiting in the car," Kristin said. "Waiting with an ulcer hoping you'll say yes."

No, Jack thought. Whatever it is, the answer is no. He was already working on excuses, a difficult process since she hadn't given him much to go on yet.

Kristin took a breath, then plunged into it. "We were scheduled to leave this morning on our honeymoon, but our Nanny just called to tell me that she's got to go watch her daughter have a benign tumor removed in Ohio."

Now that he saw where she was heading with this, Jack felt better about shaking his head. A gesture Kristin chose to ignore.

"Gregg's parents are too old, mine are too crazy, yours are dead and our tickets are nonrefundable so that leaves you," she summarized. "Please do this, Jack. Please."

"Gee, I don't know," he said, "I'm working on a story. I mean I'd love to, but—"

"You're always working on a story, Jack," she shot back at him.

"Yeah, it's what I do."

"There's only one story around here. It's the same old one," she said with a coldness that always surprised him. The only thing cold about his Kristin— the pert suntanned blonde he'd met on a press junket to Turks and Caicos and married three months later—was the strawberry daiquiri she'd been sipping. Jack remembered her standing slowly, rising from the flock of supine, bikini-clad stews; flight attendants, they called them now. Rising, with that frosty glass in her hand. It was all steamy smiles and warm coconut oil back then, with heat rising off a pair of legs that seemed to go on forever.

"It's about an every-other-weekend good-time father to whom responsibility is a dirty word," she complained now.

"A hint here, Kristin?" he said. "During an attempted manipulation such as the one in progress here, I would have gone with flattery. Tends to piss people off less, you know?"

Her shoulders slumped. "Why do I have to be the grownup while you always get to be the little boy?" she wanted to know.

The alarm clock was still beeping. He'd never fully realized how irritating the sound was. He hurried to the bedroom, calling over his shoulder, "Because in the beginning of our relationship, when we were choosing up sides, you chose grownup first. This is really how you want it, Kristin." Then scooping up Maggie, who was bouncing on his bed, he silenced the alarm with his fist.

"What I really want," Kristin said, when he returned, "is—just once—for you to make a sacrifice in your career for your daughter."

"Fine. No problem at all," Jack said, twirling Maggie. "I would love to take care of this bunny . . . this noodle girl, this bunny, noodle, Maggie Magpie . . ."

"Really?!" Kristin said. "You'll do it, Jack?"

"Abso-Maggie-lutely!" He tickled and kissed his daughter. He loved to hear her giggle.

"Find me, find me," she was laughing now.

Jack set her down. "Okay. I'm counting. I'm shutting my eyes, Maggie Mags. Go on, hide."

"Here's her slicker, Jack." Kristin folded the little

purple rain jacket over a dining chair stacked high with magazines, then began rifling through her shoulder bag. "Thank you, Jack. Gregg'll be so relieved. I've got Maggie's doctor's number here, and a really good baby-sitter's number who can help you out tomorrow. She's got a walk-on part on a soap today."

"Is she under the couch?" Jack crooned.

Kristin looked up, concerned. But Jack was talking to Maggie, who'd apparently found a hiding place.

"No!" Jack continued. "Is she . . . in the closet? No! Where is she?"

"Jack? Jack, here's the list. See, I'm putting it right here, in Maggie's backpack, okay?"

"Is she in the light bulb?" Jack asked.

"Hello, Jack. Excuse me. I've got to run. Jack, just one last thing, okay? My neighbor was supposed to take Maggie to school for me this morning. Jack?"

"What about the refrigerator?" he cooed, crawling toward his kitchen.

"She lives in our building." Kristin raised her voice. "Apartment 4B, okay? Here's her number." She scrawled the number on a piece of junk mail sitting on his hall table, then tore it off and held it out to him. But he was crawling away.

"Okay, I'm putting it down, right here. Next to Maggie's backpack. Her name is Melanie Parker. If you want her to take Maggie to school for you, bring Maggie to her house before eight so you don't miss them, Jack. If not, call Mel and let her know that you won't need her to take Maggie. Okay? Jack? I'm going to miss my plane."

Jack glanced at her over his shoulder. He put his finger to his lips, motioning for silence; then he pointed, indicating that he'd discovered Maggie's hiding place.

"Maybe I should cancel my honeymoon," Kristin suggested. "I don't think this is such a good idea."

Jack jumped up. "No, no, no," he assured her, ushering her out the door. "Don't cancel your honeymoon. We'll be fine. Go. Enjoy."

── TWO ──

The race was on. Heels clicked along the side-walks, sports shoes power-walked through the park, urban assault boots scuffed uptown. Hands—chapped, gloved, french-manicured, calloused—snatched newspapers, deposited transit tokens, clutched purses, briefcases, and laptops with practiced paranoia. A dog walker herded six straining canines across Lexington Avenue where they caused brief havoc among a gaggle of Navy-blazered parochial school students. Next door to Melanie's building, a uniformed doorman, a large black umbrella furled at his side, watched pale thin clouds scudding across the morning sky.

Upstairs, Mel waited at the open door of her apartment, toying with her beaded necklace and tapping her toe with mindless impatience. She had already smoothed down her short dark skirt, tucked in her peach silk blouse, and brushed the shoulders of her pinstriped suit jacket. She looked fine. Fine, she told herself. Businesslike, competent. Except for the hair. Mel blew it out of her eyes again. It was blonde, several different shades of blonde—most of them real, she argued with the imaginary critic who was her constant companion. And unless she tied it back in a knot or anchored it with barrettes, it tended to be a bit wild.

"Sammy, honey. I've got your lunch box. Don't forget your backpack," she called down the hall to him. "Come on, sweetie. We don't have time to fool around this morning."

He came out of his room wearing his Mets cap, backpack in place, carrying the fish bowl in two hands. "We never have time to fool around, Mommy," he said earnestly. Then he sneezed.

As he glided slowly down the hall toward her, Mel foraged in her purse for a Kleenex and the chewable Vitamin Cs she'd packed. "You cannot have a cold today," she said. "Tomorrow maybe, but not today, please."

She found the bottle and, after wiping Sammy's nose, slipped two tablets into his mouth. Then she pulled her datebook out of her big leather bag and flipped it open.

"We're going to fool around on Saturday," she promised him. "See, I'm writing it down. In between the laundromat and Foodtown. Yikes!" she said.

"The rent. I forgot again. " She found her checkbook and quickly scribbled out a check.

"That the rent?"

"Yes," Mel said, holding the check in her teeth, while she stuffed the Filofax and checkbook back into her bag.

"Can we do that thing again," Sammy asked excitedly, "where I look really sad and ask Mr. Josephson not to cash it for a week?"

"Sammy," she said sternly. "We only did that once. Because we were very, very desperate. I've got a good job now. We don't have to do that anymore, thank God. And, if my presentation goes well today, hey, maybe I'll get that raise we've been waiting for. Then we can give Mr. Josephson a real thrill, and pay him before the first two late notices."

"You look pretty, Mom," Sammy said, moving slowly past her out into the hall, careful not to tip the fishbowl.

"Does my eye look okay?"

"What happened?" Sammy asked.

"Why, can you still see it? I put enough concealer on to hide an elephant."

"See what?"

"Nothing, sweetie. I banged my eye last night. It's nothing. Sammy, we've got to hurry now. I can carry that for you."

"No, Mommy. Miss Wallace gave them to me to watch."

"I know, sweetie." Mel put her hand on Sammy's

back, gently moving him toward the elevator. "Right now we're in a little bit of a hurry because we're taking your friend Maggie to school this morning and we can't be late because of your field trip."

"I hate Maggie," said Sammy morosely. "She thinks she's *so* funny."

Mel pressed the buzzer and heard the elevator start up. It creaked and clacked up the shaft toward them. "Well, her mommy just got married, Sammy, and they have a plane to catch, so we're going to be good neighbors today."

She checked her watch as the elevator labored toward the twelfth floor and noted with satisfaction that they were only two minutes late. "If you give me the fishbowl, Sammy, you can ring Maggie's bell," she bargained with him.

He went for it. They traded. Sammy took his lunch box; Mel guarded the fish. The minute the elevator doors opened, Sammy sprinted down the hall to Maggie's door, and started ringing the bell. "Okay, enough," Mel called. "Easy does it, Sammy." They stood before the door together and waited.

"Maybe we should go," Sammy said, after a while.

Mel rang again, and checked her watch. "We can't just leave. I promised. We still have twenty-five more minutes to get to school. You don't have to be there until eight-thirty. Let's give them five more minutes."

"But my field trip, Mommy." Sammy tugged at her skirt. Mel took his warm hand and patted it reassuringly.

"Have you ever missed anything in your life?" she reminded him.

They waited. Mel's hand hesitated at the bell.

"Why don't you bang on the door?" Sammy suggested.

It wasn't as if she didn't want to. "You can't *bang* on the door of honeymooners," she instructed.

Mel's fishbowl hand was beginning to tingle. She switched the fish to her doorbell hand, and shook the tingling one. Then she shifted the little glass bowl back, wedging it more firmly against her waist.

It was eight-ten.

Sammy shuffled his feet. "Come on, Mom, no kidding, we're going to be late."

Mel knocked politely at Kristin's door. Sammy rolled his eyes at her. She gave him a lame smile, then banged on the door as hard as she could. "Kristin?" she shouted. "Kristin, it's Mel. Are you there? Hello, is anyone home?!"

At eight-twelve, Mel grabbed Sammy's hand and they ran for the elevator. With water sloshing dangerously against the fishbowl's sides, they rushed to the bus stop where a pretty young woman in a shiny black slicker was handing out cards containing tiny glass vials of a new perfume called Fireworks.

"Don't miss the Fireworks," the girl chanted. "Tonight at eight. Fireworks by Grapelli."

"No thanks," Mel said, but Sammy accepted a sample from the grateful girl as they caught the tail end of the line inching into the already packed M102.

Standing on the bottom step, as the bus doors closed, Mel tried to squoosh her hand down into the inside pocket of her shoulder bag where she kept her bus and subway tokens in a red purse. It took six blocks and four minutes of rush hour traffic for her fingers to find the little purse. "Got it," she announced triumphantly.

"Watch out!" the heavyset lady on the step above them screamed.

"Hang on! Hang on!" the bus driver hollered, then let loose a stream of prayerful curses, beginning with Mother of God and ending with an altogether different mother.

A yellow cab weaving between traffic lanes had bumped into the side of a fast-moving van. The taxi pinballed into the bus, then spun out into traffic again where, with a terrible metallic crunch, it was broadsided by a Mercedes. Steam rising from its crumpled hood, it squealed to a stop, ending up sideways across the avenue, blocking traffic from the East Eighties to Harlem.

Sammy lurched forward. Mel caught him by a strap of his backpack and, through a miraculous balancing act, managed to keep the fish from sloshing out of their bowl. "Nice save, Mom," Sammy said, as the driver ushered them off the damaged bus with a blue transfer they hadn't even had a chance to earn.

"Here, Mom," Sammy said, handing Mel the sweaty little Fireworks sample he'd managed to save.

"We gotta hurry, Mommy," he urged, as she slipped the perfume card into her bag.

"We will, sweetie," Mel assured him. "Just hang onto the fish for a minute while I fix your shoe. Your laces are open."

Sammy set down his lunchbox, took the fishbowl from Mel, and stuck out his right foot. Mel knelt before him, too rushed to worry about her skirt riding high on her thighs.

8:29 A.M.

"Great green globs of greasy grimy gopher guts," Jack Taylor sang to his daughter. Their cab hadn't budged since turning down Lexington Avenue a couple of minutes ago. Gridlock again. With a mayor as crooked as Aikens the city was lucky to have a grid left to lock, Jack thought, continuing his ditty. "Mutilated monkey meat, little babies' smelly feet . . ."

"Eeeww, Daddy!" Maggie giggled.

"Great green globs of greasy grimy gopher guts . . . And I," he prompted.

"And I . . . forgot my spoon!" Maggie shouted.

"All right!" He gave her a high five, her little hand light against his palm. "What time is your soccer game again?"

"I don't know," she said, unconcerned.

"I'll find out when we get to school." He glanced out the window. A bus had collided with a taxi up

ahead. "What time does your school start, Maggie?"
he asked.

"I don't know," she said.

He sat back. "Probably starts at nine. Almost
everything starts at nine. But we'll get there a few
minutes early just in case." Jack reached into his
trenchcoat and pulled out a handful of wrinkled bills.
"Maybe we should walk the rest of the way, okay,
Maggie Magpie? We're getting out," he told the
driver.

Taking Maggie's hand, Jack led her through the
stalled traffic to the sidewalk. "Okay, now." He
glanced up at the street sign, getting his eastside
bearings. "What street is your school on again?"

"It's that way, Dad," Maggie said, tugging his
hand.

"Good girl. Lead on, Dr. Livingston."

"Who's Dr. Livingston, Daddy?"

"A famous explorer, just like you, Baby Boo!
Maggs, hang on a minute, let me grab a paper." Jack
stopped at the newsstand and picked up a copy of
Newsday. Fishing in his pocket for change, he caught
a glimpse of a knockout blonde kneeling at the feet
of a kid about Maggie's age.

"What an adorable little girl," a pleasant female
voice said.

Distracted, Jack turned to see a brown-eyed chest-
nut beauty fluttering her lashes at him. She dropped
her coins into the vendor's bowl, and slowly chose a
New York Times.

ONE FINE DAY   33

"Thank you," he said, giving her the automatic, safety-tested grin. Girl says hello, Jack flashes teeth. Nothing to it. He turned back in time to see the blonde getting to her feet.

She shook her head the way a pony might, swinging a mane of wild blonde hair out of her eyes. It was a casual gesture, but it mesmerized him. Then she smoothed down her little navy blue skirt and straightened her jacket with an impatient tug. If she leaned over now and tried to stroke wrinkles out of her flawless sheer pantyhose, Jack thought, he'd need an ambulance.

"That lady likes you, Dad," Maggie piped up.

"Really? How can you tell?" Jack asked, astonished. Then he realized she was talking about the brown-eyed girl. He paid for the *Newsday*, decided against looking for his column right now. "Come on, Maggie, we'd better get you to school. Daddy's got a busy day." The blonde and her little boy had vanished.

"I'm going to miss the boat trip, aren't I?" Sammy said, as they turned the corner onto 85th Street. From under the bill of his baseball cap, his imploring eyes searched his mother's face for reassurance.

"Sweetie, I'm walking as fast as I can. You don't want to spill the class fish, do you?" It had started to rain, very lightly, Mel noted. She could wait a few minutes before pulling the umbrella out of her shoulderbag. They were almost at the school.

"There's no way they're going to leave on time," she assured Sammy. "You'll make it. I promise." She could see Eastside Montessori's tasteful maroon-and-gray awning a block away. "But let's run. Just in case," she decided. In her best and highest heels, she clacked through the drizzle trying to keep the fishbowl upright.

"Hooray for us! We made it," she enthused, ducking under the entrance canopy.

"Mom! Mommy! Mom, look!" Sammy cried.

Mel looked. Up ahead, a large school bus with "Eastside Montessori" emblazoned on its side was turning the corner onto Park Avenue.

"No way," Mel heard herself say. "Come on, Sammy, let's go in."

The french doors were locked. There was a colorful, child-decorated sign taped inside one of the panes.

THE WHOLE SCHOOL IS ON THE CIRCLE LINE TODAY. SORRY WE MISSED YOU.

"What does it say, Mommy?" Sammy asked.

Mel shook her head. She couldn't bring herself to tell him. She couldn't answer. She set down her black bag and the fish bowl on the cement ledge near the front door and, closing her eyes, tried to figure out what to do next.

A phrase from a long-ago song, a song about having days like this, had been buzzing in her head. In constant motion from the moment her bare heel stepped down on a flashlight battery this morning,

Mel hadn't had time to really hear the words. Now they came to her like an admonishing finger waggling under her nose—her mother, Rita's, scrupulously moisturized, french-manicured finger. If she hadn't been so depressed about spoiling Sammy's day, Mel thought, she'd probably laugh at the appropriateness of the lyric.

Mama, the merry widow Rita McKenna, had indeed told her there'd be days like this, warned her, urged her to mend her independent ways—for Sammy's sake.

"It takes two to make a child, and two to rear one," Mel's mother maintained. "You need a husband, a partner. Sammy needs a man around the house."

Easy for Rita to say. She was a cheery dynamo who had turned down two proposals of marriage in the six years since Mel's father had died. When Mel pointed out her mother's own penchant for living alone now, her full, active life—the woman was never home: she had season subscriptions to the Roundabout, the opera at Lincoln Center, the film series at the Modern, short story readings at Symphony Space; she was taking cooking and language classes; she served in a soup kitchen twice a week and volunteered at Memorial Sloan Kettering where her husband's prostate cancer had first been diagnosed—when Mel asked her, "Why don't *you* remarry?" Rita would point out in her relentlessly up-beat way, "Because my beautiful children are all grown up, dear."

Clearly, Mel was no Rita. Here it was, not nine a.m.

yet, and she was already exhausted. *Unacceptable*, the critic argued. *There is no time to be tired, this is no time to think of yourself.*

Mel took a deep breath and tried to concentrate on the task at hand: how to break it gently to Sammy that they'd, literally, missed the boat.

"The whole school is on the Circle Line today. Sorry we missed you."

Mel opened her eyes. A slightly damp, slightly familiar, extraordinarily attractive man in a rumpled raincoat was standing beside her, reading the sign aloud.

He grinned cheerfully at her. His teeth were big, white, expensive; his health insurance probably included a dental plan. His gold-flecked brown eyes crinkled at the corners, seemed amused at the sight of her. A fine mist of rain sparkled in his dark hair. "Big uh-oh, right?" he said, "I'm Jack."

Melanie blinked up at him.

"Is that what it says, Mom?" Sammy asked, upset, crushed.

"Hi, Sammy's Mommy," said Maggie.

Maggie? Mel looked down at the little girl. Suddenly everything fell into place. Including the quick irritation she felt at the big grinning dope beside her. "You must be Kristin's ex-husband," she accused.

Maggie's hair was unbrushed. Tangled, it had been rubberbanded into a little pouf on top of her head. And there was something white and viscous stuck in it. Impulsively, Mel reached down and plucked it out. It was a partially melted marshmallow. "Hi, Maggie," she said. "Did you have marshmallows for breakfast?"

The child nodded. "Daddy made s'mores. Hi Sammy," Maggie said sourly.

"Hi Maggie," Sammy scowled back at her.

"Oh my God," Jack said. "You must be . . ." He drew a handful of notes from his pocket and shuffled wildly through them. "Er, you're not Sheila, the actress-babysitter, or Dr. Alexander, the pediatrician, but . . . you're—" He waved a paper scrap under her nose. "Melanie Parker, right? You're, see, there it is, underlined three times. You must be 'Don't forget to call Melanie Parker.'"

She nodded, not trusting herself to speak.

"I'm so sorry," he continued. "We're not quite together this morning. What do you mean I must be Kristin's ex-husband?"

"Well, that's Kristin's daughter and this is a totally ex-husband thing to do," she replied, not bothering to hide her annoyance.

Jack's grin faded abruptly. "You must know, because that was a totally ex-wife remark," he said, reaching into his jacket pocket.

Feeling a frantic rush of panic, Mel racked her brain for what to do next. Suddenly, Jack Taylor's fingers were moving with an odd, annoying motion, distracting her. "Excuse me. What are you doing?" she asked snappishly. He opened his hand and showed her his palm. In the center of it was a large marble. A kid's marble. A toy!

"What? This?" he asked innocently. "It's my lucky marble."

"It's not working," she said. "Apparently."

She noticed a cab stopping down the block on the corner of Lexington Avenue. Two dark-suited businessmen stepped out. "A free cab!" she found herself shouting, seized by inspiration. Mel glanced at her watch. It was . . . oh, no, nearly 8:45! She grabbed Sammy's hand and dashed out into the street, signaling wildly. "Taxi! Taxi!" she called. A free cab at 8:45. On a rainy weekday morning. It was a sign from heaven.

The cab sped over potholes and manhole covers toward them. "Thank you, thank you, thank you," Mel chanted, climbing into the back seat and pulling Sammy in behind her.

"Hey, wait up, hang on," Jack shouted. He grabbed the cab door, waited for Maggie to scoot in next to Sammy, then shoved in behind her. "You forgot something," he announced, slamming the door. Reaching across the children, he roughly handed Mel the bowl of fish he'd retrieved from the ledge where she'd left them.

The bowl practically landed in her lap. Some of the murky fish water splashed over the edge, onto her good pinstriped jacket.

"Wow, Mom!" Sammy gasped, alarmed at her

carelessness. "You forgot the fish." He shook his head gravely.

"It's okay, I've got them now, sweetie. Thank you very much," she growled at Maggie's father, then called to the driver, "Pier Fifty-six please, as fast as you can."

— Three —

The cab jerked out into traffic. The bowl water sloshed again, almost disgorging the mean-looking red-and-gold fish—a move that did nothing to improve his temperament or her own, Mel thought, as Sammy began to wriggle against her.

"Not me, you," he was saying to Maggie.

"Cooties, cooties, cooties," the little girl chanted at him.

"Mom," Sammy grabbed Mel's sleeve, perilously jiggling the fishbowl. "I don't want to sit next to her," he whispered. "Do I have to?"

"He's got cooties, Daddy," Maggie was telling her father. "I don't want to be next to him."

"Those aren't cooties, Maggie Magpie," Jack said in a jolly voice that Mel found gratingly irritating. "Those are *cuties*. Your friend has cuties. And so do you. Upsa-daisy!" He hoisted his daughter over his lap at the same moment Mel lifted the fishbowl, allowing Sammy to crawl across her and sit by the window.

Which meant that she and Maggie's fun-loving father were now mashed together in the middle of the backseat. She glanced at him. He shot her a quick false smile and opened his *Newsday* with a deliberate flourish that left half of the paper covering Mel's face.

She waited, but he did not seem to notice this. She cleared her throat. He studiously ignored her. Finally, she hissed at him, so that Sammy wouldn't hear, "I don't know where *you* get off having an attitude. Since it's your fault both our kids might miss their field trip."

"My attitude," Jack replied, with what sounded to Melanie like a haughty sneer, "is derived from your attitude."

"*Derived*?" she snorted. "You must be a writer."

"Don't tell me. Your ex-husband is a writer, right?" He rattled his newspaper.

"No, my ex-husband is a musician," she snapped, delighted to prove him wrong.

"I am a writer, actually." Jack flashed her a little self-congratulatory smile. "A journalist," he said, moving his side of the newspaper closer to her face.

Under a photo of him—grinning, of course—was the column: *You Don't Know Jack* by Jack Taylor.

That's why he'd looked familiar, Mel thought. "I don't need to see that," she said, pushing the paper away. "I already have an opinion of you."

He shrugged and went back to proofreading his column. She looked at her watch. It was ten minutes to nine. Mel pulled her cell phone out of her bag and, after a moment's hesitation, dialed her sister's number.

Miracle of miracles, Liza herself picked up.

"Liza?!"

"This is she," Liza said, already impatient. "Mel?"

"Hi, Liza, thank God you're there."

"You sound surprised."

She *was* surprised. Usually Liza's cook, nanny, or housekeeper—all of them named Mary—answered the phone. "Mary!" Mel heard her sister shout now, "Courtney's heading straight for the Steuben vase. Grab her . . . or it . . . or something!"

"Mary, the nanny?" Mel asked.

"Yes. You can't imagine how chaotic—"

"Liza, I need to ask you a huge favor," Mel said, glancing at Jack, who remained absorbed in his own doubtlessly hardhitting prose.

"Melanie, where are you? You sound awful," Liza said. "Don't answer—I can't talk now. I'm on the other line, organizing Kyle's fun run."

"Don't hang up!" Mel begged, "I need you to—" She heard chirping noises.

"Wait," Liza said. "I'm getting kissed all over."

The chirping continued.

"Is that Davis?" Mel asked, trying to imagine Liza's conservative lawyer husband bestowing noisy little bird kisses all over his fashionable forty-year-old wife. "Liza, listen, please." She raised her voice conspicuously. "See, a typical you-know-what, who obviously thinks that a minor amount of charm replaces integrity and commitment, has ruined not only *my* day, but . . ."

Jack threw down his newspaper, picked up *his* cell phone, and began dialing. Flamboyantly.

Sammy leaned across Mel's lap. "My mom hates your dad," he whispered to Maggie.

"So?" Maggie responded, flouncing her slender shoulders. "My dad hates your mom."

"So?" said Sammy.

"Hey," Jack spoke loudly, cheerfully, into the phone. "It's me."

Hal Hartley, Jack's best friend at *Newsday*, and his office mate, shouted over a cacophony of ringing telephones and noisy banter. "Jack! Where the hell are you?" Hal was a big man, unapologetically overweight. He had a fat man's voice, husky, wheezing, and leavened with a ready laugh. "Lew's asked me six times already if I knew where you were."

Jack cut a sidelong glance at Mel. Her eyes met his, squinched up childishly, and looked away. And gorgeous cat-green eyes they were, Jack could not help noting. Seductive and steamy. There ought to be a truth-in-labeling law for women, he thought. The kind of health warning you got with cigarettes.

"Liza, if I ever act interested in another man again, please kick me," she was saying.

So she had no boyfriend. Big surprise. He'd gladly

have volunteered—for the kicker's role, of course. Not the boyfriend, poor bastard. "So tell me," he said in his best breather's voice to Hal, "I just wanted to know if you're wearing panties today?"

Sure enough, she flashed him a look of curdling disgust.

Hal laughed his wheezing fat man's laugh. "Cute," he said. "You're in big trouble with Lew."

"What color are they?" Jack asked slyly.

"Gotcha, cowboy. Someone's listening in. Okay, here's the deal. You're in deep shit on the garbage story, Jacko. Major problem."

"Pink?" Jack said.

"I'm not wearing panties today," Hal chortled. "But I hope you are, and they better be made of steel."

"I am not leaving Sammy at the Ninety-eighth Street Day Care Center, Liza," Mel said forcefully. "He hates it because a kid tried to beat him up there once. You're my sister, how can you not watch him for me? I have a presentation in fifteen minutes and you have no job, a nanny, a cook, and a house-keeper."

She'd gone too far. She could hear it in Liza's voice, which had become stiffly formal. "Mary, the nanny, is leaving to take Courtney to Mommy and Me." Liza announced. "Mary B is cooking all day for our dinner party tonight, Mary O is cleaning for our dinner party tonight. And I *am* working . . . in the school of-fice this morning."

"What about later?" Mel asked, softening her

voice. "Maybe I could switch my presentation. It's just for my boss today, but he's been hinting at a promotion and I don't want to do anything to mess it up."

"Later, I'm getting dressed," Liza said, inflexibly, "for our dinner party tonight."

"Liza," Mel tried again, "you're insulted because I said I have a presentation and that you don't work." She glanced over at Jack.

"A real superwoman," he said to his panty pal. "You know the type. Can't open her door. Won't shut her mouth."

"Excuse me," Mel whirled on him. "Are you talking about me?"

"The First Lady," he told her, flashing that ingratiating grin again. "Thinking of doing a piece on her."

Mel glared at him, while her sister rebuked her from the Olympian heights of her Fifth Avenue penthouse. "I do have a job, Melanie. I am the CEO of this household. I'm sorry I can't help you out today. But you're perfect. You'll figure something out."

"Jack," Hal said. "Listen, buddy. Mayor Aikens just called a whopper of a press conference and Lew's ready to kill you. Are you sure your source is clean on this?"

His source was Manny Feldstein, the Tevye of Roslyn, Long Island. Impeccable. Reliable. Squeaky clean. "Absolutely, sweetie pie," he told Hal. "I miss you, baby. I'll be there soon." Then he clicked off his cell phone.

"Thanks a lot, Liza," Mel said. Her sister had already hung up. She looked out the window. The cab was just pulling onto the pier. The Circle Line boat was still at the dock. "Open the door, Sammy. Get out, sweetie," she called, as Jack stuffed a careless wad of bills into the cabdriver's hand.

Jack and Maggie and Sammy ran toward the boat. With her bag in one hand, the fishbowl in the other, and her cell phone dangling from her mouth, Mel followed as quickly as her burden and heels permitted.

"Wow!" said Sammy, impressed with the bigness of the boat—which was oddly quiet, Mel thought. Almost deserted.

Suddenly, a deafening foghorn blew. From behind the white, docked boat, another Circle Line vessel appeared, brimming with screaming, happy school kids, and their smiling teachers and chaperones.

Mel's heart sank. Sammy's face fell. From the big, noisy boat, friends were waving and calling to him. He didn't wave back. He stared up at them in disbelief, in abject misery, tears beginning to brim.

Cell phone strap still clamped in her teeth, Mel turned to Jack. Now what? her face said. Do something, she silently implored. Jack tore his eyes away from her, ripped off his raincoat, tossed it over his little daughter, and ran.

"We can still make it, goddammit," he hollered,

and took off at full speed after the boat. "Wait! Wait!" he called.

It was pretty heroic of him to charge along the edge of the dock, waving his arms and shouting into the wind. Heroic, but unrealistic, Mel thought, spitting the cellular back into her bag and setting it down on the weathered planks of the pier. There was no chance the boat would stop now. Not even if someone aboard recognized Jack as not just another well-dressed, emotionally disturbed New Yorker whose Prozac had run out.

Mel draped his raincoat over her arm and pulled a hairbrush out of her bag. Carefully, she removed the rubberband and traces of marshmallow from Maggie's hair, and gently began to brush it. "Thank you," the little girl said politely. "My Daddy doesn't know how to fix girls' hair because he's a boy."

It began to really rain. Mel drew the children against her and they huddled under Jack's raincoat, while she brushed through the tangles in Maggie's hair. Behind the departing excursion boat, the cliffs of New Jersey were a smudge of gray on the horizon. Gusts of water streaked sideways, pounding the pier. Mel reached into her bag, pulled out an umbrella, and gathered the children under it.

Jack's dark curls were taking a beating, she saw. They were plastered to his head now. His lightweight wool jacket was sucking up water, growing visibly bulkier. By the time he realized the futility of his effort, Mel thought, the jacket would probably have returned to its native state and smell like a ripe sheep.

She turned back to the children. "Who wants to go on a boat in the rain, anyway?" she asked, sounding falsely chipper even to herself.

Sammy didn't answer.

"I know," she said softly, brushing his hair back with her fingers. "You did."

"I don't even care," Maggie announced, as her father trotted back toward them, wet, breathless, and altogether too gracious in defeat.

He was grinning again, that galling boyish grin that had probably won him a lifetime of reprieves. He took his sopping raincoat from her and tossed it carelessly, in a bunched rope, over his shoulder. "Look, er . . ." He checked the scrap of paper, the one on which her name was scrawled in rapidly blurring ink. "Melanie," he said, as if he'd known it all along, as if he hadn't really needed a cheat sheet to pass the test. "Look, I really feel awful about all this."

On behalf of her devastated son, Mel glared at him.

"I'm sorry, kid," Jack said to Sammy. "I'll make it up to you somehow, okay?"

To Mel's surprise, Sammy shrugged and offered Jack a shy, forgiving smile. Man-starved, Mel thought. He thinks this macho cowboy is the real deal, a regular stand-up guy. Well what's he supposed to think, he's only six years old, she reminded herself. Instinctively, she drew Sammy closer to her. Instinctively, he tried to wriggle away, to shrug off her embarrassing over-protectiveness.

"I'm hungry, Daddy," Maggie announced.

Jack dug into his wet pockets, and came up with a linty little clear plastic container. He rattled it forlornly at his daughter. "You want a Tic-Tac?"

"What, all out of marshmallows?" Mel heard herself say.

Jack ignored her. "Sorry, Maggs, that's all I've got right now."

Maggie wrinkled her nose and Jack returned the Tic-Tacs to his pocket, then opened his newspaper and held it over his head as shelter from the rain.

Melanie reached into her black bag, pulled out the buttery croissant she'd packed for breakfast and handed it to Maggie.

The child accepted it enthusiastically. "Thank you, Melanie," she said.

"You're welcome, sweetheart."

Jack was impressed. "Listen, I really am sorry," he said to Mel again. "What do you say I take care of the kids during your presentation—"

She narrowed her eyes at him.

"I overheard you," he confessed. "You've got one in fifteen minutes, right? And maybe you could watch them for me later on today? Seems the Mayor's pretty ticked off at my column today and . . ."

Maggie licked croissant flakes off her lips, then reached up with butter-greased fingers, and took her father's cell phone off his belt. Sammy immediately began foraging in the big leather bag at his mother's feet.

"Hi. Maggie Taylor calling," Maggie said. "I have an urgent message for . . ."

Sammy pulled out Mel's cell phone, eager to play.

". . . stupid Sammy Parker," Maggie concluded.

"I'm not stupid. You're stupid," Sammy grumbled.

Maggie was not impressed. She rolled her beautiful brown eyes at Sammy's weak comeback.

Incensed, he hissed, "You're the stupid one, Maggie. You are."

Sammy felt a hand on his head, and looked up. It was Jack. Maggie's dad was stroking his hair. He wasn't the least bit angry that Sammy was calling his daughter stupid, either. "So there," Sammy summarized, feeling dangerously powerful, feeling like the mightiest Morphin of all.

Jack hadn't realized he was touching the kid's head, until Melanie glanced curiously at his hand. "Sorry," he said, quickly, just to be on the safe side. Everything he did or said seemed to get under her skin. And very nice skin it was. Basically flawless, except for the rosy spots of color that rode her cheekbones when she was in high dudgeon. Judging by those spots, and an increasingly familiar glint in her yellow-green eyes, her dudgeon was rising again.

"So what do you say we help each other out?" he asked, grinning hopefully. It was a good solution, a perfect solution, Jack thought. It was not only clever, but wonderfully generous. Rain clattered on the newspaper he held over his head while he waited for her response.

He didn't have to wait long. "I don't think so," Mel said. "I only let incredibly responsible people watch my son."

"I'm incredibly responsible," Jack said. "I am," he added defensively, sounding very much like her son, he realized.

The boy sneezed. Melanie Parker reached into her shoulder bag and took out a handkerchief, which she snapped open and held over Sammy's nose while he blew. She tucked the handkerchief away and reached back down into the bottomless black bag. This time, her slender hand returned grasping a bottle of chewable vitamin C. Efficiently, she popped one into Sammy's mouth, then took one herself. Finally, she offered the bottle to Jack, who shook his head no. Not that he wasn't impressed. *Au contraire.* The woman was a walking medicine chest, a hypochondriac's wet dream.

"You were saying?" she demanded, clearly aware of her awesome performance.

"I'm incredibly responsible," Jack reiterated with less conviction.

Melanie cocked her head at him. "Well," she began promisingly. "I guess it would be an enormous help to me today."

Go know women, Jack thought. Go know. It was one of his favorite Feldsteinisms. Manny, the Mayor's snitch, was always saying it: Go know. And here was the perfect situation. First, the mercurial, blonde über-mom had made Jack feel like El Floppo the

Clown Parent, and now she was entrusting him with her son's care. Go know.

Oh no. "Wait a minute. What am I thinking of?" Jack blurted out. "I've got a shrink appointment in fifteen minutes!" Break out the grin, he told himself. Turn on the charm. "I've been going to a shrink because I chronically forget my shrink appointments."

She was not amused.

Jack reached for Sammy's head again. He settled for Maggie's. It didn't matter. He just wanted to remind this Melanie creature that he was a nice guy, a child patter.

His daughter looked up at him, then turned her attention back to Sammy. "Let's switch," she said, reaching for Mel's phone.

"Okay," said Sammy, delighted to trade his mom's cellular for Jack's leather-encased model. The sound of a motor scooter distracted him. Sammy turned to see Lyle Kleigler riding on the back of his baby-sitter's MoPed.

Lyle was wearing a red helmet and a yellow rain slicker, Sammy noticed, and he was holding onto his sitter's waist like a big baby.

"Lyle, Lyle, crocodile," Maggie began to chant as the motor scooter sloshed along the pier toward them.

Lyle, who was even shyer than Sammy, buried his face in the back of his baby-sitter's soaking wet sweater.

It was a short sweater, skinny and black, Jack noticed. It clung to the girl's curves but left her midriff bare. And the rain-drenched jeans she was wearing with her black motorcycle boots rode low on her rain-pearled hips.

Melanie watched Jack watching the girl. He was like a hound at point, she thought. Why his little wet nose was practically quivering.

The motor scooter stopped a few feet from them. The girl in the drenched sweater smiled at Jack. "Looks like we missed the boat," she said.

Jack smiled back at her.

"They left five minutes ago." Mel broke the steamy silence.

The girl seemed surprised to see her. "Oh," she said. Then, "Sorry, Lyle," she called over her shoulder. "We'll hit a flick instead, okay?" And off they rode. Jack's gaze, full of mute longing, Mel thought, followed them out into traffic.

Mel cleared her throat. Jack turned back to her, the flirtatious smile still on his lips.

"About your offer to take care of Sammy," she began sweetly. "I really don't need your help. But if I did . . ." she said, moving the fishbowl to her left hand and hiking her black bag onto her shoulder, " . . . if I was lying in the street, filthy and bleeding, if my son was cold and hungry, you would be the very last person I would turn to for help because I suspect that when it comes to what women really want and what children really need . . ."

She grabbed the paper off his head and held his

column close to his face. "You don't know jack!" Then she dropped the paper and placed the fishbowl in his hands. "These are the class fish. They were supposed to be back in the classroom at eight-thirty this morning. Now they're spending the day with you."

Mel whirled around, took the leather-encased cell phone out of Sammy's hands, dropped it into her black bag, and hurried toward the street to find transportation.

"But Mommy," Sammy called, scampering behind her.

"Phones aren't toys, sweetie," Mel said, grabbing his hand.

"But—" Sammy tried again.

"There's a bus!" Mel shouted. "Come on, Sammy, let's run."

— Four —

Inevitably, as the morning rush hour began to subside, so did the rain. In offices all over the city, workers wrung out their cuffs and hems, set their umbrellas, boots, and walk-to-work shoes aside, and readied themselves for the day. After ushering out his first patient, Dr. Peter Martin peeled off his black galoshes and turned on the humidifier in his waiting room.

It was an overheated windowless chamber, less than one quarter the size of the spacious bright office beyond. Two chairs, of a style known a decade before as "Danish modern," sat separated by a teak magazine table. The chairs, upholstered in a nubby tangerine fabric, faced a large, framed Wyeth poster which a number of Peter Martin's patients found disturbing. Some thought the scene spare and depressing. Others saw, in the gray and pink dunes, a provocative wombscape. Martin had grown used to the complaints and analyses. When patients pressed him for his own interpretation, he often responded with Freud's "Sometimes a cigar is just a cigar." Occasionally, however, he'd chuckle and remind them that a disturbing poster in a therapist's anteroom was good for business.

Peter Martin glanced at his watch. When his next patient, Jack Taylor, actually remembered their appointment, he was usually late. The doctor decided he had time to fix himself a cup of tea and make a few phone calls before officially considering Taylor's session forfeit.

In his suite's closet-sized kitchen, Martin selected a fragrant, spicy Red Zinger over the mellower blends of tea stacked in the cupboard. The rain, the hissing radiator, the galoshes he'd just removed had all left him feeling sluggish. He needed a jolt, not a soporific, to carry him through the day.

As he prepared the tea, Martin mused on the patient he'd walked to the door five minutes earlier. A troubled sixteen-year-old with enough rings piercing his flesh to qualify him as a latter day St. Sebastian. Five on one earlobe, three on the other, and one each through his lip, nostril, and eyebrows. What he'd once have treated as a self-mutilation compulsion was now a fashion statement.

Martin ran a hand through his thinning hair. It had been thick and wavy, worn down to his shoulders not so long ago. And his neatly trimmed beard, mostly white now, had been bright red and full.

He hoped Taylor showed. It wasn't the fee. He billed patients for his time whether they took advantage of it or not. No, he liked Jack Taylor. The guy was lively, action-oriented; a bit of a hero, full of himself, believing his personal ideals of right and wrong, justice and injustice, should be society's universal models. A bit of a reactor, too—defensive, defiant, impulsive—but one who reminded the doctor of his own younger, idealistic, constantly outraged self. Taylor's difficulties were in the usual slow-changing, quality-of-life areas of intimacy, connection, and responsibility.

He was carrying his old, chipped, World's Best Daddy cup through the narrow waiting room, when the door buzzer sounded. Jack Taylor? Only ten minutes late? Martin raised his eyebrows quizzically, set his cup down on the teak table and, straightening the back issues of *Smithsonian*, *Scientific American*, and his wife's old *Premiere* and *People* magazines, buzzed Taylor in.

Jack was in a lightweight jacket and drenched. A little girl, with his wet raincoat over her head, sat on his shoulders, carefully balancing a small bowl of fish.

"Jack, come in, come in," Martin implored.

"Watch your head, Maggs," Jack said, ducking into the waiting room. "Dr. Martin, I'd like you to meet my sweetie, sweet, sweet daughter, Miss Maggie Magpie."

"A pleasure," Martin said, taking the raincoat and fishbowl from the child, and helping her down.

Holding his dripping sportscoat, Jack surveyed the small waiting room. Then, as the doctor hung his raincoat neatly on a bentwood rack, Jack tossed the jacket onto the hot, relentlessly hissing radiator. "Sorry we're late. What a morning," he said, taking the fish.

"Come on in and let's talk about it," Peter Martin suggested. "Maggie, would you like to look at any of these magazines while your father and I talk?"

Maggie shook her head no.

"We'll be just inside there," Martin explained.

"Dad." Maggie took Jack's hand. "Can I come in and play with you?"

"Abso-Maggie-lutely!" Jack promised, picking her up and carrying her past Dr. Martin into the office. "What have we got for her to play with, Doc?" he asked, looking around the fastidiously ordered room.

Peter Martin searched his bookshelves and desk drawers. "Here we go," he said at last. "Maggie, look at all these funny little pictures. What do you think this is?" he asked, holding up the first inkblot card in the Rorschach series.

Maggie shrugged her shoulders. "A big mess," she ventured.

Martin smiled. "Can't argue with that," he said.

"Right you are!" Jack laughed. "A mess is the correct answer. Okay, Maggie, sit down right here on the rug next to my chair. You can fool around with those cards while we talk, okay?"

"I don't know, Jack," Martin began, softly. "It's going to be difficult—"

Jack shook his head confidently. "Piece of cake. We'll just...you know, we'll be...conscientious. Believe me, I need this session, Doc. You cannot believe what my ex—"

He looked at Maggie, who was already sitting cross-legged on the rug, busily examining the Rorschach cards. He fell back gratefully into the upholstered chair opposite Peter Martin's leather recliner. "What, er...you know who...So she just drops off the, er...." He glanced at his daughter again. "The bag of cookies," he said, tossing his head significantly in Maggie's direction. "And tells me to keep them for the week."

"How do you feel about the cookies, Jack?" Martin asked, folding his hands over his belly, and slowly twirling his thumbs.

"I love the cookies. But I have a big problem with ...er..."

"The cookie maker?" Martin suggested helpfully.

"Yes. Because the cookie maker thinks that all I'm interested in or that all I'm capable of handling with respect to the cookie in question is the...um..."

"The frosting?" prompted Dr. Martin.

"Exactly," Jack agreed. "But just because the frosting is my specialty doesn't mean I can't do more. I've got many layers to me," he asserted. "And they're not all vanilla, either. I've got chocolate inside of me. Deep dark chocolate!"

Maggie tugged at his pants leg. "Daddy, I'm still hungry," she said, staring up at him.

Jack took a calming breath. "I don't have anything with me here, sweetie. We'll eat right after me and Dr. Martin finish."

"What about the cookies?" she insisted.

"What cookies?"

Dr. Martin said, "You know, Jack. Cookies, cookies . . ."

"Oh, *those* cookies. don't have any on me, Maggs. In a little while, we'll get something."

"Okay." Maggie nodded and went back to playing with the inkblots.

"I can't tell you how sick I am of these . . . angry, resentful . . ." Jack resumed. "Er, you know . . ." He cast an eye at Maggie, then glanced at the little fishbowl on the end table, half hidden by the Kleenex box. "Fish," he decided. "These, um, fish who think you owe them, but who won't trust you for a second to do anything for them."

"There are other fish in the sea, Jack," Martin said with a twinkle.

The door buzzer sounded. "Excuse me, Jack. That'll be my next patient." The doctor moved to his desk and pressed the little release buzzer that opened the waiting room door. "She's early. We still have time." He returned to his recliner. "You were saying?"

"Yeah, I was thinking . . . I'd like to meet a fish who wasn't afraid of my dark chocolate layer," Jack said. "You know what I mean? And of course, she'd have to love my cookie. But I think my ex-cookie maker has turned me off to all fish. I met a real piece of work this morning."

"Tell me about her," Dr. Martin said.

"Well, I've got to admit that this fish was a fox. She's got her own cookie, too. But what a . . . female dog, if you know what I mean. I mean, she just shoved her fish in my face—"

Dr. Martin was aghast. "In front of your . . . cookie? What was *she* doing with fish anyway? Is she AC/DC?"

Jack paused. "Er . . . What are we talking about here?"

"Fish with fish in front of cookies," Dr. Martin said.

It took Jack a minute. "No, no, no! Not, you know, lady fish with lady fish." He pointed to the glass bowl. "*FISH* fish!"

"Oh, I see," said Dr. Martin.

"Jesus Christ, what's that stench?!" came an angry voice from the waiting room. "Did a goat die in here?"

"Who's that, Daddy?" Maggie asked, alarmed.

"My next patient, Maggie," Dr. Martin said. "Jack, you left your wet jacket on the radiator, didn't you? Is it wool?"

"One hundred percent," Jack said.

9:30 A.M.

Thirty blocks in under thirty minutes. From the pier at Forty-third Street to the puddled canyons of lower Park Avenue. "How about we try out for the marathon next year?" Mel gasped at Sammy, who was trotting easily along beside her.

They had jumped off the downtown bus at Fourteenth Street and waited five minutes for the crosstown bus to appear. When it did, it was bulging with miserable, wet, sullenly belligerent people, who completely ignored the harried bus driver's command to "Step in, step in, step to the rear!" So Mel had hailed a passing gypsy cab and paid five dollars to listen to salsa music and stare out, beyond the pungent gold deodorant crown on the dashboard, at the hopelessly snarled traffic. Finally, she'd bolted. She and Sammy had leapt from the oversized, underheated brown car and charged on foot toward her workplace.

Outside the revolving door of the renovated Arts and Architecture Building, Mel stopped to catch her breath. She had a stitch in her side. Her stockings were spattered with mud. The rain, and now the ceaseless drizzle, had destroyed her hair. Sammy, on the other hand, wasn't even breathing hard. And he'd made the run with a knapsack on his back, a lunchbox in one hand, and a small green rubber monster wearing a purple cape and horned mask in the other.

"Sammy, put that away now. Here, give it to me,

I'll hold it," Mel said. She reached for the toy, but was waylaid by a smudge of dirt on Sammy's cheek. She spit on a tissue and began to scrub the spot.

"After you," a courtly baritone said. Mel looked up. A tall man in a well-tailored raincoat was holding the revolving door for her.

What was it that that Jack jerk had said? A real superwoman, you know the type. Can't open her door, can't shut her mouth.

"No. After you," Mel replied, quickly tucking the tissue back into her pocket.

"I insist," said the gentleman.

"I insist more." Mel matched his courtly smile, tooth for tooth.

The tall man shrugged and entered the building. Mel finished cleaning Sammy's face. He squirmed under her hand. "Mommy, how come you don't want to go in?"

"I'm going, I'm going," she said. "And I can certainly open my own door—especially a revolving door. Here, give me what's-his-name."

"Gorgon."

"Give me Gorgon and let's go."

"I want to play with him." Making a loud buzzing noise, Sammy flew the action figure out of Mel's reach.

"Play quietly," she said.

They hurried through the lobby and entered an empty elevator. Mel's shoulder ached. She put down her black bag and instantly snagged her pantyhose.

With a grunt of disgust, she reached into the bag, pulled out a package of new pantyhose and tore it open. "Now, listen, Sammy, when we get upstairs," she said, standing behind him, wriggling out of the ruined stockings. "You've got to be really, really quiet." She shoved the old pantyhose into the bag and slipped on the new pair.

"Okay," Sammy said. He spotted an old soda can standing in the corner of the elevator and tentatively touched it with his toe.

"Super quiet, okay. Don't touch that," Mel said.

Sammy withdrew his toe and set Gorgon buzzing again.

"I know I can count on you, sweetie. I've got a really important meeting. If this goes well—"

"We buy a cushion!" Sammy exclaimed.

"We'll *have* a cushion," Mel corrected him. "Then I'll breathe easier *and* have more time with you."

Sammy shrugged and continued his sound effects.

"I mean it, Sammy. You can't even make one peep." She pointed at the little green action figure. "And he can't make a peep, either," she said.

Whirling, with Gorgon in his hand, Sammy knocked over the can. A whoosh of warm, still fizzy, soda spilled everywhere.

"Don't even think about it," Mel warned, as Sammy started to test the sticky brown liquid with his foot. She yanked him away from the puddle just as the doors opened.

"Uh-oh, Mr. Leland isn't going to like this," Eve-

lyn, the receptionist, remarked the moment she saw
Sammy step off the elevator. She peered at the boy
over the top of her glasses, then cocked her head at
Mel, waiting for an explanation.

"Luckily, Mr. Leland doesn't have to know everything," Mel said, walking Sammy across the pristine
expanse of bleached elm floor that stood between the
elevator and Evelyn's imposing desk.

With her pen, the receptionist pointed at the clock
mounted on the paneled mahogany wall behind her.
"He knows you're late," she responded dryly.

Mel let it slide. She had to get Sammy settled, preferably out of sight, before she could begin to deal
with Smith Leland. She walked Sammy to the area
behind Evelyn's desk and began digging in her bag
for things to keep him occupied. She pulled out a box
of non-toxic crayons, a puzzle book, and a net bag
full of emergency toys. Stuck onto the toy bag was
the little perfume sample Sammy had picked up this
morning. She took it off and dropped the toys at
Sammy's feet.

. "Wow, there's my Ninja soldiers," he said excitedly. "Oh, boy, Mom, and the car!"

"Now remember what we said in the elevator
about being really quiet," Mel reminded him.

Sammy nodded, absently. He'd already pulled
open the bag and was busily unloading GI Joe,
X-Men, and Ninja Turtle action figures, Matchbox
cars, his electronic Game Boy, and his prized shiny-

red, remote-control hot rod with its gold flames and detailing.

Evelyn couldn't believe her eyes. "Excuse me. What are you doing? You can't leave him here," she fumed.

"Mr. Leland doesn't have to know about this, does he?"

"He doesn't have to," said Evelyn, "but he will. Last summer when Sally Hanson's kid had poison sumac, she stopped by the office for under two minutes. Mr. Leland smelled calamine lotion and took the rest of the day off."

"I know, I know," Mel said. "Look, Evelyn, I have a meeting with Mr. Leland in . . ." She glanced at the clock. "Oh God, ten minutes ago," she said, alarmed. "It's an important meeting. The most important meeting I've had with him since I came to the firm. I've spent months designing this shopping center, weeks slaving on the model. It's perfect. It's smart. It's good design. It's form-follows-function. I have just about killed myself on this model and it's hopefully going to get me a promotion and Mr. Leland will—"

"You're not following me," Evelyn interrupted. "This is not your basic easy-going, child-friendly type person. This is a man," she said slowly, "who looks the other way if his cab should happen to pass F.A.O. Schwarz."

"I realize this," Mel capitulated. "But I have no choice today. Evelyn, he is not sick and he doesn't have poison anything. He's a very, very good little boy who is just going to sit here behind your desk and play with his toys very, very quietly."

Sammy marched his Ninja Turtle across Evelyn's desk over a set of blueprints. Mel grabbed the Turtle, sneaking a quick peek at the pages.

"The Haskell blueprints. Rob Wilding got them in three weeks ahead of schedule." Evelyn confirmed Mel's apprehension.

"He did?" Wilding and she were neck in neck for the associate position Bradley Marks had recently vacated. The Yates shopping-center project was her big chance to pull ahead. "Three weeks early?" she murmured.

Evelyn smiled her assent.

"Five minutes, Evelyn," Mel begged. She ran her fingers through her hair, and smoothed down her skirt. "That's all, five minutes. I promise."

Evelyn squinted up at her. "And I would be doing this because . . . ?"

"Because of our sense of solidarity?" Mel suggested.

Evelyn was unyielding.

"You know we're both women and this is a tough office—" she continued desperately, "and a tough world for working women who, you know—"

"Five minutes," Evelyn rasped.

"Have some . . . Fireworks," Mel said, winging the sample onto Evelyn's desk.

The receptionist brushed the little card into her top

drawer. "Already got two. Girl at the subway station was giving them out."

Mel grinned and nodded. "What every woman needs, right? More Fireworks. Thanks, Evelyn. He'll be so good you won't even know he's here. Isn't that right, Sammy?"

She looked down. Sammy's upper torso was disappearing beneath Evelyn's desk. "Sammy!" Mel called. She got to her knees and began tugging at his belt. "Sammy, what are you doing?" she hissed. But she could see for herself now. He was steering his remote-control car toward Evelyn's stockinged foot.

"Mom!" he asked, suddenly. "What are those things all over—"

Mel clamped a hand over Sammy's mouth and hauled him out. "Those are corns," she whispered, trying to keep the exasperation from her voice. "Evelyn will put her shoe back on in a minute. But you have to be quiet, sweetie. It is sooooo important."

She stood up and straightened her skirt again. Smith Leland, the patriarchal, Pritikin-thin head of the firm, was marching down the hall toward them. He did not look happy. Mel was grateful, but not entirely relieved, to see him veer off into the conference room where, he had every right to believe, she'd be waiting.

"Oh my God," she muttered. Then turning to Evelyn, she said, "Mommy's got to go talk to Mr. Leland now."

"Good luck, Mommy," Evelyn called, as Mel hurried away.

"Good morning, Mr. Leland." Mel stuck her head into the conference room to see Smith Leland sitting alone at the head of a lacquered oval table. He was twirling his thumbs. Leland's impeccable gray suit and crisp Oxford shirt enshrined a trim body fastidiously exercised. His gray-streaked hair was slicked back and neatly barbered. Everything about him was placid, orderly, controlled. Except his slender patrician thumbs and his face, which twitched impatiently at her.

"Let me just go get the model," Mel said, with a grimace she hoped would pass for a confident smile. "I'll be right in." The diagrams and figures she'd gone over last night were in her big black bag. Mel set the bag down, patted it nervously, and retreated.

She hurried to her cubicle a few doors down from the conference room. On her drawing board sat the architectural model of the shopping center she had designed. It earned her first genuine smile of the day. No one, not even Mr. Leland, could fail to be impressed and excited by it. Mel stared for a moment at the scaled-down structure, with its graceful promenades and shops, allowing the sight to quiet the anxiety and turmoil of the morning. Then, calm, sure of herself again, she picked it up as proudly and carefully as a master chef preparing to present a peerless souffle.

A miniature car cruised down the corridor. Coming out of her office, with the large, detailed model in her hands, Mel didn't notice it. Her eyes were on the door to the conference room, just ahead. She was trying to measure it, trying to figure out whether the model would fit through it straight on, or whether she'd have to edge in sideways, which would make for a much less dramatic entrance. Sideways, Mel had just about decided, when the little red car caught under her toe, knocking her off balance.

"Oh no, ohmigod, ohmigod," she cried, teetering precariously, the model shifting dangerously in her hands.

Down the hall, she could see Sammy, peering out from under Evelyn's desk, the telltale remote still in his hands. His mouth flopped open at the sight of her. His hazel eyes were almost comically huge. Suddenly, he squeezed them shut, and drew his head into his neck like a turtle. That was the last Mel saw of him before the model flew out of her hands, and she fell backwards, arms wildly pinwheeling.

If Leland heard the crash, he chose to ignore it. Mel was on her hands and knees, silently keening over the broken model when he called from the conference room, "Ms. Parker?"

"Coming," she said, scrambling to her feet. She gathered up the model and shoved it back into her office. Then, brushing herself off, she hurried back to the conference room. Smith Leland was rearranging the Sulka paisley handkerchief in his breast pocket when she entered. Still seated, still impatient, still waiting at the long, sleek oval table, he pointed his patrician chin at her. "The model?" he said.

Mel gave him a big, cheerful smile and moved to the table. Striking a businesslike pose, she laid her sticky palms on the lacquered table top and leaned forward earnestly. "Yes, well, I'm sorry, Sir," she said, racking her brain, thinking as fast as she could. "I forgot, um, the model is still in the model shop downtown. I'm, er, heading there right now."

Out of the corner of her eye, she thought she saw Sammy's apparently indestructible red car again, heading into the conference room. "See, I stopped by there earlier this morning to pick it up for this meeting, this very meeting," she told Leland. "Uh, that's why I was a bit late." She blew a fallen lock of hair out of her eyes. "Because the shop was, um, locked." The unrepentant car continued to move toward her.

Like a frog's tongue lashing out suddenly to catch a fly, Mel's foot jerked out and stopped the car. She wriggled it under the table, clamping it firmly beneath her shoe. "I promise you," she said, eyes wild with panic—which, she could only hope, Leland would construe as fierce sincerity, "that you're going to love the model, Mr. Leland, Sir. And tomorrow at five o'clock, the people from Yates and Yates Construction are going to love it, too."

"Yes, yes, well," Leland said crisply. "The presentation's been changed to today at two. You'll be ready?"

Something brushed against Mel's leg. Mindlessly, she swatted at it. "No problem, Sir. None at all," she assured Smith Leland, then, glancing down, she saw Sammy trying to pry his car from under her foot. She reached under the table and began gesturing frantically, trying to shoo him away.

"What is it?" Leland demanded suddenly, peering around the conference table to find out what was going on.

Mel flashed her eyes at Sammy, then converted her warning look to a delighted smile. "What an adorable little boy," she cooed. "Hi there! Hi." She fluttered her fingers at him.

Leland clicked on the intercom. "Evelyn, would you check that my Amoxicillin prescription still has refills available? If not, call Dr. Berman. And bring me my pitcher of distilled water," he growled. "I've got to take a pill. Immediately. Oh, and bring the Haskell blueprints, too, as long as you're coming."

Mel leapt up and grabbed Sammy's hand and tried to pull him out of the room. But he resisted. He wanted his car which, it appeared, Mel had finally put out of its misery. "Mom, I want—" Sammy protested.

She clamped her hand over his mouth. "That's right. Let's go find your Mommy," she said, almost bumping into the suddenly efficient Evelyn, who'd appeared at the door with Leland's water pitcher in her hand.

"I'm very sorry, Sir." Evelyn cast an accusatory

glance at Sammy, then turned the water pitcher upside down to illustrate her point. "All your distilled water has been spilled onto the Haskell blueprints."

"Do you know that every Thanksgiving I catch strep throat?" Leland asked wistfully. "Children that are perfectly healthy can give you strep throat from other children they know without you even going near them." He pulled his Sulka handkerchief from his pocket and shook it out. "My sister sets up a children's table in the next room and I still get strep throat," he said, putting the handkerchief to his mouth and glaring at Sammy.

Sammy glared back. Mel grabbed his hand and cleared her throat. Assuming a take-charge attitude, she announced: "We're going to find his mother, Sir." She grabbed her leather bag and slung it over her shoulder.

"She must work in those new law offices across the hall," Leland ventured.

"I'm sure she does," Mel agreed, nodding her head at Sammy, encouraging him to nod yes, too. He just stared at her, bewildered, betrayed. "Come on, little boy," she said with a tight smile.

"And, Ms. Parker?" Leland added.

"Yes sir?"

Mel's cell phone rang. "Excuse me just a second," she urged, reaching into her bag and retrieving the phone. "Hello?"

"You're in for it now, buddy!" a husky voice rasped. "Major press conference today at five."

"What?" Mel said.

"You sound funny, Jack," said the stranger. "Bad connection. Call me back." Then slyly, the voice added, "And Jack . . . I put my panties back on." The man heaved a guttural, wheezy laugh into Mel's ear.

Confused and disgusted, Mel hung up immediately. "I'm so sorry," she apologized to Leland.

He was staring at Sammy, who suddenly sniffled almost imperceptibly. "You know what I think of when I look at him?" he asked. "Carrier monkey."

Mel tried to chuckle. "He's not a carrier monkey, sir. He looks like a very healthy little—"

Sammy, glaring at Leland now, suddenly unleashed a deep, phlegmy cough.

Leland recoiled in horror. "Just make certain that the model is properly lit for this afternoon's presentation," he insisted, drawing a travel-size container of Listerine from his breast pocket and spraying it into his mouth. "We're only going to make one first impression, you know. And I'm counting on you to make sure it's a brilliant one."

"Yes sir." Mel grabbed Sammy's hand again. "Let's go find your mommy now," she said sweetly. "I'm sure she misses you." She led Sammy down the hall and into her own cubicle. He stared up at her, a look of grave accusation on his face.

"I had to do it," she whispered defensively. "I'm sorry. I'll tell him about you when you're in college." The destroyed shopping-center model was on her drafting table. She turned her attention to it, biting her lip as she studied the damage. "God, what am I going to do?" she muttered.

Sammy flinched and hung his head.

"It's totally ruined," Mel said.

"I'm really sorry, Mommy." Sammy's voice broke. He looked up at her, his glassy doe eyes irresistibly remorseful.

"It'll be okay. We'll just fix it," Mel said. Then added uncertainly, "Somehow."

Sammy's eyes began to brim with tears.

"Oh, Sammy, sweetie, don't cry." Mel knelt down and took him in her arms. "It really wasn't your fault." She thought about the strange phone call she'd gotten in the conference room, the raspy voice and gloating laughter. Jack, the guy had said. "No, it's not your fault," she repeated with sudden conviction. "It's Maggie's daddy's fault."

— Five —

The Four Brothers Coffee Shop was just around the corner from Dr. Martin's office. By the time Jack arrived with Maggie on his shoulders, the briefcase crowd had come and gone. They'd ordered their coffee and eggs-on-a-roll to go, or wolfed down their toasted corn muffins and tossed tips into the juice spills on the Formica-topped tables.

Administrative assistants had nearly emptied the mints from the metal saucer next to the cash register; white mints filled with bright dabs of jelly. Accountants and sales managers had taken most of the toothpicks. Junior execs had exited with packets of Sweet 'n Low lining their pockets. By the time Jack said, "Whoopsa-daisy," and sailed Maggie down to the floor, the only white collar left in the place belonged to Benny, the short-order cook.

Still the Four Brothers was packed. Tired truckers

and cabbies streamed through the door, intent on cleaning their thick chipped plates of steak and eggs and rubbery stacks of pancakes. Puffy-eyed artists and actors hunched over steaming mugs of coffee. Poets toyed with toast. Anyone not actively engaged in conversation, read. Damp newspapers, mostly.

A hostess with burgundy nail polish and dyed black hair led Jack and Maggie to a corner booth and gave Jack a flirtatious smile with his menu. Jack broke out the grin, and the woman blushed appreciatively.

Their waitress was wearing a short-sleeved shirt, black pants, nurse's shoes, and a lot of makeup. It was hard to tell her age. But the plastic tag clipped to her belt said Veronica. Her pupils, shaded by mascara-laden lashes, dilated when she saw Jack. "What'll it be?" she asked hopefully.

Jack smiled at her. Veronica gave him a grateful wink. Not wanting to disappoint her, he ordered a bacon cheeseburger, fries, and a chocolate milkshake. Maggie decided on oatmeal.

"Dad. You know, your coat is really smelly," she said, when Veronica left them to find a bottle of ketchup for Jack.

"Smelly, belly, peanut butter and jelly?" he replied.

Maggie giggled, then shook her head at him. "No, really."

"It's 'cause it's wet," Jack said. "Soon it'll be dry and good as new. Want me to hold your nose till then?"

"Da-ad," she drawled, "you act so silly."

"What's wrong with silly?" Jack asked. "No crime in being silly. You think we could have a two-party system in this country, or even a decent President, if we outlawed silliness?"

Maggie shrugged, then busied herself fingerpainting in a sugar spill. "That isn't a very good breakfast, Daddy," she said when their food arrived.

"That's one of the privileges of being a grownup," Jack explained, pouring ketchup on his cheeseburger. "You can act like a kid whenever you feel like it." He took a bite of the burger, and wiped a trickle of grease from his chin.

Maggie watched. "Mommy would never let me eat hamburgers and milkshakes for breakfast," she said.

"You see what I mean?"

"No," she said, as Jack's phone began to ring.

He unhooked it from his belt and clicked it on. "Hello?"

"Who's that?" a woman's voice asked.

"Who's *this*?" Jack demanded.

"This is Rita McKenna. What are you doing with my daughter's phone?" the woman asked. An edge of fear had crept into her voice. She'd tried to mask it with icy hauteur.

"Er, Rita?" Jack looked suspiciously at the cell phone in his hand. Close, but no cigar. His had a leather casing. This one did not. This one was . . . "Oh, no," he grumbled into the phone. "We must have switched them."

"Switched what? Who is this? Where is my daughter?" Rita wanted to know.

"It's okay. No big thing. I'm Jack Taylor," he said, trying to calm her. "Our kids are in school together."

"*You Don't Know Jack*, Jack Taylor?" Rita asked, surprised, pleased.

"That's me." There was that grin again. Hear a happy woman, see a pretty girl, flash a Taylor grin. So what? he thought. He liked her voice. She was probably a nice person. Probably a white-haired innocent who'd never intended to spawn a vengeful she-devil. At least Rita had known who he was. She'd recognized his name immediately; at the very least, she'd read bus ads for his column.

"Oh my God, you are so adorable. I love your column. You alone are going to nail that S.O.B. mayor of ours, aren't you?"

"Well," said Jack modestly, "I'm going to try."

"You married?"

"Divorced, er . . ."

"Listen, Jack. Hold on a minute. I've got to go get exfoliated. Jack, Melanie's got your phone, right? Give me that number."

He obliged.

"All right, darling. I've got it. Listen, Jack, if you talk to her first, do me a favor. Her sister called me here to see if I could baby-sit Sammy later on, but I'm in the middle of my Spring Spa Day at Elizabeth Arden's and it's too late to cancel now. Otherwise I would love to have baby-sat, because no matter what she thinks, I have forgotten all about Sammy putting my wedding ring up his nose."

"I'll tell her, Rita," Jack promised.

"You're adorable," Melanie Parker's mother said, then hung up.

Maggie was experimentally pouring a steady stream of sugar into her oatmeal, watching the white granules dissolve and sink. "Daddy, who was that?" she asked, when Jack clicked off his phone.

"That was your friend Sammy's mommy's mother."

"Sammy's a doo-doo."

"Probably not his fault," Jack said. "A lot of guys are doo-doos. Hang on a second, I've got to call the probable cause of his doo-dooism. Are you going to eat all that?"

He dialed his number, then reached across the table and scooped up a spoonful of Maggie's oatmeal. "Mmmm-mmm," he said, only momentarily deterred by sugar shock. "Dee-luscious. Almost as sweet as you."

Maggie laughed.

"Answer," Jack told the phone.

Mel answered. "Hello?" she said.

"Hi, it's Jack Taylor."

She was instantly outraged. "How did you get this number?" she demanded.

Jack shook his head. What a piece of work, he thought, rolling his eyes, automatically trying to enlist sympathy, as if Hal were sitting across the table from him and not his six-year-old daughter—who sensibly ignored him. She was breaking off bits of toast and dropping them into the fishbowl. "That's my phone you're holding," Jack told Rita's bad seed.

There was silence while she verified the information, he assumed. Having checked the phone and realized it was his, she returned with an irritable, "This is so typical of you."

How crazy was he? He'd actually—briefly to be sure—entertained the idea of mentioning how lively and intelligent her mother had sounded. It had even crossed his clearly unreliable mind to let her know that his own folks, Mary and Phil Taylor, late of Roxbury, Mass., were three-thousand miles away, turning to vintage leather on the groomed links of the golf course attached to their Palm Springs retirement villa; the condo his sister Maura's husband—Henry, the real-estate mogul—had purchased three years ago as a time-share investment.

He'd toyed with telling her she was lucky to have family so near, and that sometimes he missed his. "Could we possibly bypass the hostility and just do messages?" he said instead.

"Fine," Mel said.

"Great. Your mother's in the middle of her Spring Spa Day and can't baby-sit and wants you to know that she is not still upset about Sammy sticking her wedding ring up her nose."

"*His* nose," she snappishly corrected. "Thank you. You have a press conference at five."

"Thank you," Jack snapped back.

"Goodbye." She hung up.

Jack glanced at Maggie while he redialed his number. "Those fishies look pretty well fed," he told his daughter.

"Hello?" Mel was back on the line.

"Shouldn't we arrange to switch back our phones?" he suggested amiably.

"Tomorrow morning when we drop the kids off at school," she snarled. "On time." Without waiting for his reply, she clicked off.

"Maggie, when you grow up," Jack said, clipping the cellular back onto his belt. He reached across the table and took his daughter's hand. "When you grow up, and you are incredibly beautiful, searingly intelligent, and possessed of a certain hidden sweetness that becomes like a distant promise to the brave and worthy—" He gazed soulfully into her young eyes. "Can you please not trample to shreds and beat to a miserable pulp each and every poor guy who comes your way just because you can? Can you please not do that?"

"Okay, Daddy," Maggie said.

"Thank you," said Jack. But there was a strange little grin on her face that told him she was not being entirely honest. Inside her, Jack suddenly suspected, was the seed of just the sort of woman he feared.

"Check please," he called.

"For you," Veronica responded with a comforting wink, "anything."

10:45 A.M.

In the rattling taxicab hurtling down Broadway, Mel tossed the leather-encased phone back into her bag, and grabbed the broken architectural model teetering on her lap. "Excuse me!" She tapped the plastic shield dividing her from the driver. "Could you take it easy, please?"

"You said you vas hurry," growled the driver, whose name, printed on the hack license, was missing all its vowels.

"Yes. I am in a hurry. But you have no shock absorbers. And I have a very important and valuable piece of work back here. And I cannot afford to have it banged around any more than it already has been."

"Bull-bustah," the driver grumbled, swerving viciously around a wooden barricade set up in front of an epic pothole.

Mel glanced over at Sammy. He was staring out the window. The rain had stopped, but the day was still gray and overcast. "Sammy," she began. "Promise me that when you grow up, you'll—" He turned and raised his head. His eyes were clear and innocent, staring up at her expectantly. There wasn't a hint of macho arrogance in his gaze.

"Never mind, sweetie," she said, stroking his soft cheek. "I know you'd never—"

The cab bounced past old warehouses whose street-level floors had been converted to trendy restaurants, boutiques, and galleries. Then it wheeled west, bumped along a cobblestoned alleyway, and screeched to a halt before an industrial loading dock.

Mel shoved the fare into the little drawer in the bullet-proof plastic partition. The necessity of protecting a driver from a customer wishing him harm seemed more apparent to her today than usual. Her anger, as it had a nasty habit of doing, turned quickly to guilt, and won the driver an additional dollar. She thrust it into the fare drawer and, getting a firmer grip on the model, prepared to ease out of the cab.

The taxi door opened magically. A rugged, earnest face appeared, followed by a hand still bearing traces of paint. Mel looked up into the intense, flirtatious eyes of a downtown Samaritan, an artist, no doubt. "Let me help you with that," he said, studying her legs now, with an amused smile. There was a trace of foreign accent in his voice—French, she guessed— and a wedding ring on his extended hand.

"That's okay. I can get it," she replied.

He reached in and grasped the model. "Please."

Mel held it firmly. "Really. I've got it," she insisted. Which, she thought, was much better than, "Go home and help your wife with the dishes, buster."

Charmingly, the painter stepped aside and, with a sweeping gesture, allowed her to struggle out of the cab on her own. As she passed, he muttered, "Stupid American woman." Then he got into the taxi and slammed the door.

Mel didn't want to think of the bonding conversation the painter and the cab driver might have. It was ridiculously grandiose to imagine they'd waste their time discussing her. Still, she could feel her cheeks reddening. And her ears felt hot.

"That guy called you stupid, Mommy," Sammy said, following her up the iron steps of the loading ramp.

"I am stupid sometimes," she said, then added under her breath, "I'd just rather be stupid than sorry."

"What do you mean?" Sammy had heard her.

"I meant safe than sorry," she quickly corrected herself. "It means . . . Sometimes you have to act a certain way, even if someone else thinks you're being stupid or tough or mean." She rang the bell to Vincent Wong's studio and hollered into the intercom, "It's Mel, Vincent. Help!"

"And you like to be safe than sorry, right, Mom?"

"I sure do, sweetie. That's why I always plan ahead. Like phoning Vincent before we just rushed down here—"

She glanced at her watch. Where was he?

In the single, long minute it took him to buzz her in, she ran through multiple disaster scenarios. When she'd said she'd be there at ten-thirty, had Vincent thought she'd meant ten-thirty at night? Had he nipped out to the deli for a pack of cigarettes? And gotten mugged? Or been run over . . . by an irate cab-driver, maybe, with no vowels in his name? A cabbie who was so busy commiserating with his current passenger about how unreasonable and controlling American women were that he hadn't seen Vincent Wong step into the road?

"I know, I know, you're in a hurry." Vincent said as he watched Mel lumber up the last flight of rickety wooden steps to his fourth-floor loft. He took the model from her hands, while she caught her breath. "Don't tell me this is . . . ?"

"Yup, it's Sammy." Mel nodded her head. "Sammy, this is Vincent Wong. You haven't seen him since you were little."

"Not little no more," said Vincent. "Looking good, Sammy. Okay, let's take a look at the patient." He set the model on a work bench thick with plaster dust in the center of his studio and began methodically, silently, circling it.

Mel held her breath and glanced back and forth between Vincent's calm Asian face and the squashed shopping-mall model. She'd known Vincent since her days at Pratt, when they'd taken a Methods and Materials course together. Normally, she found his contemplative approach to crisis a soothing counterpoint to her own raw nerves and manic energy. He approached problems with the confident peacefulness of a Zen master. He moved with quiet deliberation. Sometimes she'd fall hypnotically into his benign, deliberate rhythms and pace.

Not today. Today, she had no time to admire Vincent's excruciatingly slow, tai-chi waltz around the table. She wanted him to assess the damage, tell her it was no problem, and repair the model—preferably in under an hour.

"So what did you do?" he said at last. "Throw it against a wall?"

Vincent's studio was filled with pieces in progress, stacks of splintery dowels and boards, sharp fragments of metal, saws, X-Acto knives, razor blades, and containers of noxious varnishes, paints, and thinners. Sammy, surveying the loft as if it were the Soho branch of Toys 'R' Us, stretched out his arms and began swaying like a human airplane.

Mel reached out automatically, and put his arms down. "How bad is it?" she asked Vincent, without missing a beat.

"It's completely ruined. This whole middle section, from the parking lot to the pergola, will have to be redone."

"The presentation is this afternoon at two," she said.

Vincent began walking around the model again in his meditative tai-chi way. Sammy, scraping his high tops through the plaster and sawdust on the cement floor, started to shuffle after him. Mel grabbed Sammy by the collar. "Sit," she ordered, redirecting him to the chair in front of Vincent's computer, and handed him a pocket video game from her bag.

"Well, it's modular," Vincent reflected. "So it's conceivable I could lift out that damaged section and replace it with the same piece from the mock-up. That way I wouldn't have to start from scratch."

He brought over the flimsy, unadorned prototype of the shopping center they'd worked on. It was the final model's embryonic twin. "That's brilliant, Vincent!" Mel said.

From his chair, Sammy called, "I'm thirsty, Mommy." Mel dug a juice box out of her bag and handed it to him.

"It won't be perfect," Vincent cautioned her.

"That's okay," Mel decided. "Hey what's perfect, anyway? Life's a compromise, right?"

Vincent raised an eyebrow at her. "It's not even fall," he said with a little smile, "and you're turning over a new leaf?"

"What's that mean?"

"Come on, Melanie. I know you—"

"Mom," Sammy hollered. "I can't do the straw part, Mom. It's stuck."

Mel reached over and popped the little plastic straw through the juice box foil.

"—You aren't going to be happy with less than perfect, Mel," Vincent continued.

"Today I will be. I don't even want to imagine my life if I don't have that model by two this afternoon."

"Alright then," Vincent said, clapping his hands together with as much enthusiasm as she'd ever seen him muster. "Let's do it."

"Vincent?" She followed him over to a work table near the windows. "We've known each other for a while."

"How's almost ten years?"

"No," Mel gasped. "Where did the time go?"

He looked over at Sammy, who was stirring his juice with the little straw Mel had poked through the container. "That took some time," Vincent pointed out. "Feeling introspective?"

"Me?" Mel laughed. "Never. I'm your basic action figure."

"Superhero?"

"Ninja Mom," she agreed. "Superwoman." She thought of Jack Taylor. Actually, she'd *been* thinking of Jack Taylor. "Have I changed?" she asked Vincent now. "Seriously, am I hard, you know what I mean, have I become tough, insensitive, unresponsive?"

"Insensitive, you? Unresponsive?" He had poured plaster into a pail. Now he began adding water to it, very slowly. Without looking up from the task at hand, he continued in his even, methodical voice. "Melanie, even your antennae have antennae. You are the most responsive human being I've ever met. I mean, just look at you and Sammy. In the past fifteen minutes, you've occupied him with toys, you've rescued him from disaster—mine as well as his, thank you." He chose a wooden spoon from a jar filled with utensils and began stirring the mixture. "You've provided juice, set limits, and given him attention and love. You've been sensitive and responsive to his every mood and move."

"Oh, Vincent, thank you," Mel said, mindlessly sweeping plaster and sawdust from his worktable into her hand.

"So what's up? You met a guy?"

The question startled her. Yes, she almost said. Then, she laughed. "I guess you could say that. I met a guy alright. This morning." She rolled her eyes. "A real—" She glanced over at Sammy who seemed totally absorbed in stirring his juice with the little plastic straw. "A real Eddie," she mouthed. "You know, great looking, killer smile, snappy patter—totally self-absorbed, irresponsible, egotistical . . ."

"Yup," Vincent said. "Sounds like your kind of guy."

"Past tense," Mel assured him. She carried the plaster dust to the trash bin and brushed it off her hands. "Anyway, even if I liked this man, which I don't," she said, returning to the table. "Even if I found him attractive—"

"Which you do."

"Well, objectively, yes. But he ruined Sammy's day . . . which is complicating mine beyond belief." She was pacing now, looking for something to occupy her. "Sammy would be having the time of his life on a boat in the Hudson right now, sailing for West Point . . ." There was a pile of balsa wood on the work table. Absently, Mel began sorting the pieces, aligning the scraps according to size. " . . . if not for this guy's inexcusably self-absorbed behavior. But the point is, I haven't got the time or energy for . . . anyone anymore—"

"Who is he?"

Mel shook her head, waved away the question.

"Nobody, nothing. He's not important. He's the father of a schoolmate of Sammy's. He's, you know, an ex-husband."

"'Name of?'"

"Jack Taylor. Vincent, you would not believe the . . . the nerve, the, the . . ."

"*Chutzpah*?" Vincent suggested.

"Exactly!"

"Jack Taylor who does the *Newsday* column?" he asked, wiping his hands on a crusty stained cloth.

"You know him?"

"Not know, read. *You Don't Know Jack*, that's him, huh?"

"What gave you the hint?" Mel asked sarcastically. "Was it the self-absorption or the *chutzpah*?"

"Actually, I guess you could say the guy's got *chutzpah*. He's got guts, anyway," Vincent replied. "Have you been reading his stuff lately? He's taking on Aikens."

Mel glanced over at Sammy. He was sitting in Vincent's computer chair where she'd put him. He'd apparently tired of the video game and was squeezing the apple juice box, creating a little fountain of juice that spurted through the top of the straw, and dripped down his thigh onto the cushion of the chair.

"The mayor, yes, I know," Mel called over her shoulder as she rushed to Sammy. "And, no, I don't read his column. I don't have time to read it. I barely have time to—" She took the near-empty juice box away and wiped up the spill.

"Sammy, go wash your hands, please," she said. "In there." She pointed him toward the bathroom door. "I've got to make some phone calls."

When he'd gone, she said, "Excuse me, Vincent," and found a quiet corner of the loft where she murmured a quick prayer—Please, please, please, please, please . . . just this one time, please—and dialed her ex-husband's number.

On the thirteenth ring, Eddie picked up.

"Hi, it's Melanie," she said. She could hear laughter and musical riffs being played. And someone coughing, and someone else calling, "Break's over."

He was in a recording studio. She could practically smell the cigarette smoke and the stale coffee warming in a pot outside the engineer's booth. She could almost see the musicians, guys mostly, taking their break. They'd be lying around on the little leather couches outside the recording booth, or stretched out on the industrial-carpeted floor.

There were female voices in the laughter she heard. Backup singers, maybe. Girlfriends probably. She'd have been there once. Before Sammy, she used to stop by after school or work when Eddie had a recording session. She'd walk into a roomful of chain-smoking women—girls, really, with long hair and high breasts and tight pants and short skirts—waiting. Band widows. Although most of them were girlfriends. The real widows stayed home taking care of the kids and the laundry.

When had she stopped going to the studio with

Eddie? After they'd married, she guessed. After she'd met the real wedding-ring wives, and Eddie had told her that her presence got the guys uptight. Apparently, they worried about whether she'd say something, whether she'd slip and mention to Marilyn, Daisy, or Laura who she'd seen Gus or Buddy or Sandy with.

After she and Eddie were married, especially after Sammy was born, she didn't belong at the concerts, club dates, or recording sessions anymore. And she didn't want to be there, either. Part of her was always waiting for Marilyn, Daisy, or Laura to slip and mention who they'd heard Eddie was with.

Been there. Done that, Mel thought, and Eddie said, "Mel, hey, what's up? You okay?"

She took a deep breath. "I'm fine. Just fine, Eddie. I—"

"You sure are. There was never any disputing that, was there? You are one fine woman, but listen, I'm in the middle of a session, here. I gotta go. Call you back later?"

"Eddie, wait. Please. I'm not fine. I'm really not. I'm . . . Look, Eddie. I have a major presentation at work today and . . . well, Sammy's with me, and I need someone to look after him. The presentation's at two—"

"Mel, I'm in the studio today," he cut her off.

"Look, this is incredibly difficult for me, but you are the absolute last person I can think of to ask."

"Mommy, there's no towel," Sammy called across the loft to her.

She put her hand over the phone. "I'll be right there, honey." She saw Vincent toss Sammy a rag from his work table. She was about to protest, but stopped herself. "Eddie," she whispered into the phone.

"I'm recording today," he said.

"It's just for an hour. From two to three. I could lose my job, Eddie," she whispered.

"No can do," he said.

Vincent was working feverishly—for him—on the model. Sammy had discovered a furniture dolly and was just climbing onto it, tentatively testing its possibilities as a scooter.

"Fine," Melanie said. "Are you coming to his soccer game?"

"Hey, soccer. Sammy plays soccer, huh? What a cool guy."

"Yeah. He's a really cool guy," she said, feeling tears of frustration begin to well. "Okay. Try to make it, please. Central Park at six. He's counting on you."

She clicked off the phone. Sammy, steaming along on the furniture dolly, was heading blindly toward Vincent. "Sammy!" Mel shouted.

He turned, a look of stricken guilt on his face. The dolly crashed right into Vincent, knocking him forward. He lurched into the model, but braced his hands against the work table and, miraculously, managed not to destroy anything.

"That's it!" Melanie lost it. She charged across the loft, grabbed Sammy's arm and yanked him off the dolly. "What is the matter with you?" she demanded. "You almost broke it again! Why can't you just play quietly and stay out of trouble for five minutes? Don't you realize how important this is? I'm going to have to take you to the Ninety-eighth Street Day Care Center right now."

"But it's scary there, Mom. I got beat up last time. Those kids are mean."

"No they aren't." She tossed her cell phone and his electronic video game back into her bag.

"Yes they are," Sammy insisted. "You don't know." His lower lip jutted sullenly.

"Then you're just going to have to be really brave," Mel said, taking his hand. "We'd better go," she told Vincent, "and let you do your work."

"Give me an hour." He walked over to them and ruffled Sammy's hair. "Come back when there's no emergency, okay? You can help me build a model."

"Really?" Sammy said. "Can we, Mom?"

Mel nodded. Vincent took both her hands in his. "You're still my cactus-flower girl," he said with a smile. "Spiney and tough on the outside, but inside— pure, sweet milk."

— Six —

"I want some milk, Dad," Maggie said, as the elevator doors opened.

"You've got it." Jack stepped into the newsroom carrying Maggie and the fish. "There's a whole container of milk next to the coffee machine. We'll get some in a minute."

"Ooóoh, isn't she cute? Hiii, Jaaack," Marla, the young redheaded receptionist, crooned, handing him his messages. Jack set Maggie down, and put the fishbowl on Marla's desk.

"Hiii, Marla," he teased, slowly spinning her around in her swivel chair.

In the familiar manner of supermodels selling hair care, Marla tossed her adorable head, lofting shimmery ginger curls in Jack's face. "Stop," she complained, giggling.

"Okay," he said, playfully imitating her giggle.

"See you later, Marla." He took off his raincoat.

"Oooh, Jack," she said, "that jacket. Wow, you smell soooo earthy."

On the way to his office, he checked the messages, flicking through them awkwardly with one hand. "Milk department's way down there, see, across from my office," he told Maggie. "But let's go get rid of these fish first, okay, Maggie Magpie?"

"Hiii, Jaaack." With an armful of papers and file folders, a pretty girl dressed in downtown black, from her turtleneck and micro-mini to her shapely tights and lace-up boots, moved past them in the corridor.

"Hi, Jessica," said Jack, breaking out the grin again.

"I didn't know you had a daughter. She's beautiful," the girl said. "She looks just like you."

As they wound their way through the labyrinth of desks and cubicles in the newsroom, Maggie tugged at his jacket. "How come all the ladies are talking to you like that?" she wanted to know.

"Like what?" he asked, lighting up again for Doris Bass, the paper's doyen of culture, who was hard at work, a telephone cradled against her neck, her fingers industriously clacking on her keyboard. She saw him at the door to her cubicle and, returning his smile with a silent kiss, continued her phone conversation.

"Like, you know. Hiii, Jaaack," Maggie sang his name.

"Hiii, Jaaack," Celia Leonard, a willowy reporter with an anchorwoman hairdo and a *Baywatch* body, called to him.

"Hey, Celia," Jack said.

"See? See, Daddy?" said Maggie.

"Shhhush," he told her as Celia approached them.

"You know, Jack," she said in her most voluptuous drawl. "I'm doing a story on men like you."

He was beaming at her. "Really? What's the hook?"

Celia stuck a finger under one of the damp lapels of his jacket and tugged it toward her seductively. "Oh, just a little expression my mother used to say: 'Love your guy like a little boy,'" Celia whispered, "'and he'll grow into a man.'"

"Nice," Jack said. "I like that."

She patted his lapel back into place. "Honey, you're so wet," she said coquettishly. "And, nothing personal, but that gorgeous jacket of yours reeks like a goat."

"Sheep," he corrected her as she walked away. "Why does everyone keep saying goat? It's wool. Hundred percent." With a shrug, he walked into the office he shared with Hal.

The big man was hunched over his computer terminal, the cuffs of his denim shirt rolled up for action. His flying fingers added to the chaotic din of the newsroom. Jack put the bowl of fish on top of the beat-up old file cabinet behind Hal's desk.

"Maggie, I'd like you to meet my best buddy,

Hal," he said, stripping off his jacket, and flinging it onto a coat rack filled with baseball caps. He transferred his lucky marble from the jacket to his pants pocket. "Hal, this is my daughter," he added proudly.

Hal Hartley swiveled to greet them. His great flushed face took in Maggie with genuine delight. "Hey there, sweetheart," he said to her. "It's about time I finally met you." He hauled himself to his feet. "So you're Maggie the Magpie."

"Margaret Elsbeth Taylor," Maggie murmured.

"Well, Miss Taylor, it's my pleasure, I assure you. Want to see something funny?" Maggie nodded, and Hal motioned her to the open drawer of a file cabinet. "Ssshhh," he cautioned, "come look in here."

Maggie stood on tiptoes and peered into the drawer to see a plump, gray cat curled up sleeping.

"That's Lois Lane," Hal explained. "She lives here in the newsroom. You want to pet her? Go ahead. She won't bite." Enchanted, Maggie reached in to pet the old cat. "So, Jack." Hal waggled his eyebrows mischievously. "You look pretty good for a dead man."

"What are you talking about?" Jack took his lucky marble from his pocket and began rolling it around in his hand.

"Lew's been in here six times already looking for you. And pissed off doesn't begin to describe his mood—"

"I knew it," Jack grumbled, looking down at the

marble in his hand. " 'It isn't working,' she said. She's a witch."

Hal was confused. "Who?"

"This woman I met this morning. At Maggie's school—"

"She was that ugly?"

"Whoa, no. That's what makes her so dangerous," Jack explained. "She's a knockout. Little blonde with these eyes . . . yellowish eyes, you know. Yellowish, greenish . . . like a cat. Cat's eyes. And these amazing poufed-out lips, great lips. You wouldn't believe lips like that could spit out such venomous crap. She called me an ex-husband," he added indignantly.

"Oh my." Hal wrung his hands in mock horror. "*Hello*, are we talking about a female here? One of those softer, rounder people—the kind you usually peel off your socks like fabric softener strips?"

"Hal, you do laundry?" Jack teased.

Hal hung his head. "I'm a flawed man. Of course, if I were you, Jack, I'd never have to look at a box of Tide again. Never need to hoard quarters or . . . Uh-oh. Did I say Lew had been in here looking for you?"

"Six times, you said."

"Make that seven." Hal quickly swiveled his chair toward his computer and began typing, his broad back to the door.

Jack turned to see Lew Wilder, the editor-in-chief, storming toward him. Lew stopped at the door to their cubicle. He opened one of his clenched fists to rake his kinky gray hair, and the other to motion abruptly for Jack to follow him. With a doubtful glance at his lucky marble, Jack did.

"I guess you want me to watch your little girl for you?" Hal Hartley muttered.

"He probably does," Maggie said.

With Jack racing along behind him, Lew charged through the newsroom to his office. He waited, gripping the doorknob, until Jack entered, then Wilder slammed the door shut. The frosted glass rattled.

"What?" Jack said.

He could see that Lew was about to explode. The editor's thick black brows were bunched like thunderclouds. His lips were thin with rage.

"Okay." Lew perched at the edge of his desk, staring blackly at Jack. "What happened?"

"What, what happened?"

"The kickback piece. The Aikens story. You don't know what happened?" Lew growled suspiciously.

Jack shrugged. "I wrote the best story of my career?"

Lew smiled without amusement. "Very funny," he said coldly. "Who told you the Mayor's been taking kickbacks?"

"Manny Feldstein. He's been my top guy at City Hall all year."

"From the Mafia he said?"

"You know Manny's solid, Lew. He's the Assistant City Comptroller. He knows. So what's going on?"

"Manny Feldstein told you on the record that the

garbage collectors are paying off the Mafia who are paying off the Mayor?"

"Yes. On the record," Jack said.

Lew's anger was unmitigated by this information. "Because we don't like to print things that aren't true, Jack," he growled.

Jack nodded. "I'm aware of that, Lew."

"I've got sources at City Hall, too, Jack. And my sources tell me that your source is going to say that he never talked to you."

Jack's mouth flew open. "What!!?" he hollered. "No way. Can't be. I was with Manny last night, for Chrissake. I danced with his bowlegged aunt till nearly two in the morning, Lew! What the hell is going on here?"

"Maybe you're a lousy dancer. Maybe you stepped on her toes and she told Manny to sell you out. I really don't know, Jack. All I do know is that during the Mayor's press conference today at five, Manny Feldstein is going to say you made the whole thing up!" Lew grinned his icy grin again. "You didn't make the whole thing up, did you, Jack?"

"No. I swear, I—"

"You haven't gone Lone Ranger on me again, have you, Jack?" Lew said, cutting him off abruptly. Wilder pushed himself off his desk. The soles of his shiny leather loafers hit the floor hard. Even muffled by the bright blue carpeting, the sound, the quick movement, startled Jack.

"Absolutely not. I—"

Wilder was in his face. "This isn't like the time you crossed three police lines in one night, supposedly chasing your dog, and I had to bail you out of jail, Jack, is it?"

"That was a great story. You even—"

"Remember Cardinal O'Brien's cataract surgery? You posed as a doctor—"

"Lew, I should have gotten a Pulitzer on that one."

"Listen to me! Listen, Jack," Lew yelled. "You've got until five o'clock today to either get Feldstein back on the record or find another reliable source to confirm what he said. Otherwise we're printing a retraction."

"You can't!" Jack began.

"Yes . . . I . . . can! And I know a nice little paper in Jersey looking for a retired reporter. I'm goddamned sick and tired of you and this bullshit cowboy attitude of yours, Jack. I printed a story, your story Jack, basically saying that the Mayor is handing out lucrative sanitation contracts to known mobsters. I put myself, this paper, the whole damn multi-goddamn-million-dollar corporation that pays my salary and up until today paid yours, in a very shaky position, Jack. And I will most assuredly print a groveling goddamn retraction—as well as your obituary—if you don't get confirmation or a source willing to go on record by five . . ."

Lew glanced at the Rolex his family had given him

a month ago for his sixtieth birthday. "Five o'clock," he repeated. "That gives you five whole hours!"

"Give me a break, Lew," Jack said.

"Out!" said Lew.

Malcolm Briar, one of the bullpen sportswriters, and his junior sidekick, Carlos Rose, shook their heads sympathetically as Jack exited Wilder's office and started through the newsroom. Here and there a faint smile followed him, or a murmured, "Tough break, Jack." He ducked back into his cubicle.

On the blue carpet, Maggie was coloring quietly. He didn't know where Hal had found the crayons. Art Department maybe. He was on the phone now. Jack hurried to his desk and dialed Manny Feldstein's work number. There was no answer. Finally, Manny's voice mail picked up. "Hello, you've reached the office of the Assistant City Comptroller. Emmanuel Feldstein is not avail—"

"Where the hell are you?" Jack growled while Manny's voice droned, then slammed down the phone before the announced beep. Hal was still talking on the phone. Jack shook his head, sighed, then punched redial. Tethered to the phone console by its curled plastic cord, he paced impatiently through Manny's entire message. After the beep, he said in a restrained tone, one meant to be conversational, "Feldstein, this is . . . you know who. Call me . . . please. Right away . . . please. It's important that I . . . Please get back to me fast. Okay, thanks."

He hung up, took a breath, then howled, "Shit!" and punched redial again.

Maggie looked up.

"Shoot," Jack amended, flashing her a quick smile. He paced through Manny's message again, studying the cell phone on his belt. Then he said, "Manny, it's me, you know who. I'm not at my regular number today. Call me at this one." He repeated the number, then hung up.

"That bad?" Hal said, getting off the phone at last.

"Not good," he confirmed. "Manny's backing out on me. I can't believe it. He's been my guy all year. Now I've got no source for the story. I'm swinging in the wind, here. I've got to talk to him, find out what's happening. Have you heard anything? Can you make a couple of calls for me?"

"Daddy," Maggie said, "Lois is very hungry." The plump gray cat was lazily circling the fishbowl on Hal's desk. "We better get her some milk."

"Can do," Hal told Jack, punching a number into his phone. "Why don't you get the kid some milk, and I'll see what I can dig up?"

He hadn't been gone five minutes. When he walked back into the office with a paper cup full of milk, Hal said, "So, story is, Manny Feldstein is pretty much locked inside the Mayor's office."

Jack set the milk down in front of Maggie. "Thank you, Daddy," she said without looking up.

"They've got him, Jack. You can't get to him," Hal concluded.

"Shi—Shoot!" Jack said, banging his fist on the desk.

Maggie looked up.

"What? I said 'Shoot,' " he assured her, and she returned to her coloring. "I can't believe this. He must have had a complete nervous breakdown."

Hal leaned back. His leather chair creaked ominously as his weight shifted. "Either that or he doesn't want to get killed by the mob."

Jack shook his head. "I am so fuh-uh-fudged," he said, instinctively reaching for his marble.

"No doubt about that, Jack," Hal agreed. "You are definitely fudged."

"Um, Dad?" Maggie called to him.

"Not now, sweetie," he said.

"But Daddy, that cat Lois Lane—" she tried again.

"Give her the milk, Maggs," Jack said distractedly.

"She's probably not hungry anymore. She—"

"Wait," he told her, rolling the marble in his fingers. "Feldstein's been my guy all year," he said, pacing again. "I took his niece to Cirque du Soleil. I danced with his Aunt Ida, for Chrissake. The woman has two left feet, both of them size twelve. I even watched him play Tevye in dinner theater and now he does this to me." He threw himself into his chair. "Help me think this out, Hal."

"Right. So from the top, what've we got?"

Jack dropped the marble back into his pocket and pulled out his notepad. "So from the top—" he said, beginning to swivel his chair back and forth. "Feldstein told me ... 'A big guy named Sal makes monthly cash payments to the mayor's re-election campaign fund,' " he read.

"Uh-oh," said Maggie.

"Uh-oh is right," Jack concurred. "But I've got it right here. Word for word," he said, smacking the pad.

"It's your word against his," Hal said, "And since the mayor has an enviably high public opinion rating while you've got a reputation for being something of a cowboy—"

"I got to hear cowboy from you too?" Jack cut him off.

Hal pushed himself out of his chair and lumbered over to the file cabinet, where Lois Lane was licking her paws. He moved the cat aside. Her feet were wet. "All I'm saying, Jack, is that you've got less than five hours to the press conference and no other leads," Hal said, wiping his hands on his snug size-44 khakis.

"It's going to be alright," Jack decided suddenly. "It's always alright. And what is it with Lew and all these threats? Who's he going to replace me with?"

Hal pulled a Baby Ruth bar from the file drawer and peeled back the wrapper. "Frank Burroughs?" he suggested.

Jack leapt up. "Fffrrrank Burroughs?!"

" 'Frankly Speaking' is a very popular column,

Jack." Hal severed half the candy bar in a bite, then chewed raptly.

"Frank Burroughs is as overrated as his newspaper," Jack declared.

"You think the *New York Times* is overrated?"

"Lew hired me because I write for people like myself who want to know it fast and easy. I'm the guy who'd rather use two small words than one big one any day of the week. *Frank Burroughs*," Jack sneered.

Hal set down his candy bar, and pulled a newspaper off the top of the file cabinet. "Here, listen to this," he said, riffling through the pages. "Okay, here. 'While other women tried to achieve beauty with the money their rich husbands lavished upon them, she achieved it with one strand of hair across her brow.' "

Jack shook his head. "He could've said it in three words, 'She was hot.' Done."

"Lew had lunch with him last week."

Jack drew himself up with finality. "I am not getting fired, Hal. I've got alimony, shrink bills, very old college loans to repay, and a devastating plumbing situation at home."

"Don't mind me . . ." They turned to find Celia sipping a cup of coffee at the door. "Go on, please."

"Celia. How long you been listening? Want a bite?" Hal offered her the candy bar stub.

She ignored him. "I've got friends in high places, Jack," she crooned, running a hand along her thigh.

"Why wouldn't you?" said Hal, his eyes softening at the sight of her, his nostrils widening as if he could inhale her.

"You're sweet." Celia bestowed a perfunctory toe-curling smile on him, then turned back to Jack. "I mean, sources . . . those kinds of friends. I grew up in Queens—Long Beach. Sal country."

"No kidding?" Hal said, "I'd never have pegged you as a bridge and tunnel type. You seem so—"

"Excuse me," said Jack. "Thank you, Celia. Anything you can get I'd be extremely grateful for. Now, where were we?"

"Right," Hal said, reluctantly turning his attention back to Jack. "So who else can you get to open up? No other disgruntled City Hall staffers talked?" Hal asked.

"They all talked," Jack said. "But none of them had anything to say."

"I've got something to say, Jack," said Celia.

He glanced at her impatiently. "Yeah?"

"I've noticed that you haven't been dating for quite awhile," she drawled. "We've all noticed. So I've been thinking. I know you're sensitive, but frightened. I'm gentle, but brutal. Think about it." Celia smiled. "Think about me, Jack." Then she turned slowly, deliberately, on her mile-high heels and left the office.

"I will," Jack called after her. To Hal he said, "Brutal?"

"No one has ever talked to me like that in my entire life," Hal brooded. He finished off the Baby Ruth, shaking his head.

"Not dating? Am I not dating? You know, she's right. I thought it was just because of this story. I've been chasing it for months. But that's not true. It's been . . . a long time."

"Tell me, Jack," Hal said, still musing on the possibilities of Celia's brutality, "you think it's because you're good-looking or what?"

Jack laughed. "I don't know. Sometimes I think it's because of the thing that happens to my face when I smile." Jack demonstrated the grin for Hal.

"That's good," said Hal, genuinely impressed.

"I know." Jack went to the coat rack. Dropping his lucky marble back into his sportscoat pocket, he thought of Melanie again. He had tried the grin on her. "It's not foolproof," he amended, putting on his jacket. "So, listen, I'm going to head down to City Hall. Feldstein's like a couch. Once I find him, all I have to do is sit on him."

"Where are you going?"

"I'm going to go find Manny, Tonto, and I'm going to make them all regret the day that Jack Taylor rode into town."

Hal turned back to his computer. "Right," he said.

Jack hurried out to the elevator bank and shouted at an attractive woman, who was just boarding the car, to hold the door for him. He shot her the grin and was glad to see it still worked on normal females. They chatted all the way down to the lobby.

He held the door for her, then rushed out.

He was halfway down the street when he stopped in his tracks. Hurriedly, he retraced his steps back through the lobby, up the elevator, empty now, and down the newsroom halls to his office. Hal was gone. So was Maggie. Jack stuck his head out into the hall, hoping for a glimpse of them. He saw Hal talking with Carlos Rose at the sports desk near Lew's office. He was alone.

"Maggie," Jack called into his office. He crouched down and peered under his desk, then Hal's.

"Hi, Daddy." She was in the corner, between the wall and the file cabinet, playing with the cat.

"Hi, Daddy?" Jack repeated in disbelief. "I almost . . . You could have . . . Do you do this with your mother? This disappearing act?"

Maggie shook her head no.

"Because," Jack continued, lifting her up, "it's not a good thing to do. Now listen, I've got to go talk to this guy downtown," he said, carrying her out of the office. "And it's a pretty tricky thing, and I've really only got one shot at it and what I'm trying to tell you here is that . . . that . . ."

"That I can't come," Maggie said matter-of-factly.

"That's right." Jack squeezed her, and carried her out to the reception desk. "Marla, there's been a mix-up and I've got a different cell number just for the day. So if anyone needs me, it's—" He read the number off Mel's phone again.

"Sure thing, Jack," Marla said flirtatiously. She waggled her long nails at Maggie.

"Now," Jack said to his daughter, as the elevator arrived. "What am I going to do with you?"

— Seven —

They lunched in the sunlight in front of Vincent's loft. Legs hanging over the edge of the loading dock, they sat side by side on the sheet of corrugated cardboard Mel had found in the hall on their way downstairs. Sammy ate his peanut butter and jelly like a condemned man. Mel poured the rest of the milk from his Stargazer Thermos into his cup. "Think you could eat any slower?" she asked, only half teasing.

"You said to chew. You always say chew," Sammy shot back at her. His skinny shoulders slumped forward sullenly.

Mel handed him the cup. "Sweetie, if I could think of any other solution, I would. But I'm all out. I've got to get back to work. Today especially. You remember, Sammy, that cushion you talked about earlier. Hey, if Vincent does his stuff, and I razzle-dazzle the Yates boys, we're halfway there."

"Can't I go to grandma's?"

"She's not home today, sweetie. And I called Auntie Liza and she's busy, too—"

"Hey," he said, brightening suddenly. "Mom, hey, I got a idea. Let's call my Daddy."

It was Mel's turn to slump. "I did, Sammy." He stared at her, alert now, questioning her with those big, clear eyes. "He can't," she murmured, wiping away his milk mustache. "He's in the studio. He's got to play his drums today."

"Yeah, but he's coming to my soccer game, right?"

With a tissue, Mel swabbed out the milk cup and snapped it back onto the Thermos. "He's sure going to try," she said, with strained cheerfulness. She closed Sammy's lunch box and stuffed it into her black bag. "Okay, off we go—" She got to her feet, then pulled him up. "Ninety-eighth Street here we come."

The day care center was in an old building with an adjacent, fenced-in play yard, between Amsterdam Avenue and Broadway. Mel could feel Sammy's fingers tighten on her hand as the building came into view. It was a gray, unfriendly-looking place, Mel agreed, pressing down the urge to change her mind, change her life, get her resume updated, and move on.

She squeezed Sammy's hand, reassuringly she

hoped, and hurried him past two old men sharing a bottle near the metal play yard fence. Alcohol fumes emanated like heat from their stale clothing and weather-cracked lips. They smelled like arsonists, Mel thought, wondering if they were drinking lighter fluid. It was hard to tell. Only the clear neck of their bottle was visible, poking out of the brown paper bag their swollen fingers passed back and forth.

Mel's heart sank. But excited play yard voices, the sight of two attractive young women wheeling baby carriages, and a dapper elderly man striding down the street helped ease her conscience. She stopped at the bottom of the day care center stoop and looked at her watch. It was digital. She reached into her bag once more.

"Look at this watch." Mel drew out her old watch and showed the numbered face to Sammy. "Where's the four?"

Resentfully, he showed her.

"And here's the six, okay? Now, look, see this little hand? When this little hand gets between the four and the five, that's four-thirty. I'll be back—and then we can go to your soccer game!"

Her forced enthusiasm fell flat. Sammy wasn't having any. He looked up at her with a face full of eloquent accusation.

"Look, Sammy. See? I'm going to set the alarm, and you wear it." She placed the big watch onto his heartbreakingly slender wrist. "I'll be here for you by the time it goes off. I promise."

"I don't want to go in there," Sammy said resolutely.

"But it'll be fun." She was trying really hard now. She could hear the hysterical edge creeping into her fun-filled voice. "Look, it's Superhero Day!" she fairly shrieked.

This information had come to her first in the form of a sign on the fence which announced in crayoned block letters: Wednesday Is . . . Superhero Day! And from two little boys in the play yard who were chasing and threatening each other—one in a Spider-Man costume, the other done up as the Incredible Hulk.

The boys banged into the fence, sending the two old men into a bottle-saving frenzy. The boy dressed as Spider-Man was the first to notice Sammy and Mel. "He can't come in here!" he shouted, pointing at Sammy. "He's not a superhero!"

Mel straightened up abruptly. "Oh yeah?" she challenged. "You guys sure about that?"

Apparently, they weren't. But after consulting each other, they decided to test Mel's authority. "He doesn't look like one!" said the Incredible Hulk.

"He looks like a poo-poo cry baby," Spider-Man agreed.

Sammy was staring at them anxiously, his hands grasping Mel's leg. She could feel his nails biting into her tights. But this was no time for vanity. She could pick up another pair later, Mel reminded herself, at the drugstore on the corner. Now, she steeled herself and scrunched her eyes at the boys.

"Guess that shows how much you know," she replied. "This happens to be his street disguise." Lowering her voice dramatically, she added, "I just hope Super X-Man Space Ranger Sheriff didn't hear you." Then she grabbed Sammy's hand and walked him up the steps.

The first classroom they entered was empty. Everyone seemed to be out in the yard for Superhero Day. As she exited the classroom with Sammy in tow, Mel saw a father and daughter engaged in quiet conversation at the end of the corridor. The sun shone through the yard door behind them. They were silhouetted against the light. Walking toward them, Mel heard the man say, "Now when the big hand gets to here and the little hand gets to here . . . then?"

The little girl's dark profile looked adoringly at her dad. Mel found herself moved, melting at the clear sense of trust and love in the child's upturned face. "Then . . . you'll be back," she heard the little girl say.

The man took off his watch and gently slid it onto his daughter's wrist. "Now you wear Daddy's big watch," he said.

The girl's voice was tiny, troubled. "But I don't have a costume," she said.

Mel and Sammy were only a few feet away now. "Maybe I can help," Mel ventured.

The man stood abruptly and turned toward her. He smiled gratefully. It was a dazzling, irresistible smile, Mel thought. It was . . . Jack Taylor!

"Oh," Mel gasped.

"Hi," said Jack.

"What are you doing here?" she demanded, taken aback.

"I overheard you this morning telling your sister about this place," he answered, still smiling at her, but mischievously now. "But didn't you say you'd never take Sammy here?"

Mel cleared her throat defensively. Then gave up the notion of justifying herself. "Well, I got desperate," she admitted.

"Yeah, me too," he said.

Jack Taylor had a wonderful face. His soft brown eyes were appealing and expressive. There was even a hint of vulnerability in them, an openness that reminded her, just now, of Sammy's dewy innocence. Why hadn't she noticed that before? It was the grin, Mel decided. Something happened to the man's face when he smiled. Something both boyish and seductive, she realized, and disconcertingly contagious.

"So—" Mel found herself cautiously grinning back at him. "It looks like we need two superheroes and fast," she said.

The man was diabolical. Here she was smiling at the arrogant cause of the day's disasters. Abruptly, she stopped grinning and returned to business. Kneeling down, she set her bag between Sammy and Maggie, who seemed visibly relieved to see each other.

"I hate this baby place," Sammy said.

"It's fudged," Maggie agreed.

Mel could feel the run that Sammy's nails had in-itiated zip along the back of her pantyhose. Ignoring it, she rummaged in her bag, and began pulling out supplies, which she handed up to Jack. She found Sammy's Superman T-shirt, packed for after soccer; her torn black tights which could be transformed into something Batman-ish; rollerskating kneepads left over from last weekend; and, finally, her Disaster Pouch in which, she thought she remembered, was not only a pair of scissors and a roll of tape, but a silver thermal "space blanket," the kind they gave out in Central Park to runners at the end of the Mar-athon.

"Where do you get a satchel like that?" Jack asked, peeking into the awesome black bag.

Ignoring the question, Mel drew out her makeup kit and began converting the two slightly dazed faces into masks of terror. Jack was impressed, amazed, but not half as delighted as were Maggie and Sammy when Mel took out her compact and showed them how they'd been transformed.

"Now if those mean boys give you any trouble," Mel instructed Sammy, "first go to the teacher and if she doesn't help, call me on the mobile, and if you can't reach me, call 911, okay?"

"Or," Jack told Maggie, "just kick the mean boys really hard."

With some hesitation, but unwilling to show fear while the other was watching, Sammy and Maggie walked valiantly out into the play yard. Mel and Jack watched silently for a moment, then turned and left together.

"Thanks for doing that," Jack said.

Mel shrugged. "Sure. It's hard enough being a kid."

They had paused at the bottom of the steps, outside the center.

"Yes, it is," he said, too sincerely.

"And you would know," she grumbled under her breath before she could stop herself.

"What was that?"

"Nothing," Mel quickly assured him, brushing a bit of lint from her jacket.

"You've got a run in your stockings," he said aggressively.

"I know." The winos were still up against the schoolyard fence.

"You know what my mother used to say to me?" Jack asked, as Mel watched one of the men slide very slowly to the ground. The moment his descent ended, he reached up his hand for the paper bag. Reluctantly, his partner handed him the bottle. "She'd say," Jack continued pointedly, " 'Love your guy like a little boy . . . and he'll grow into a man.' "

Mel turned to him abruptly, confused. "She knew back then that you were gay?"

He took a step back. "What do you mean, gay?" he snapped. "I'm not gay." His fingers dove into his pocket for the marble.

"Then why did your mother advise you on how guys want to be loved?" she asked, irritated at his snappish tone.

Jack twirled his lucky marble. "Maybe she was hoping that one day I would find a woman like that," he impatiently explained.

"You know, I really can't stand people who blame their worst traits on everyone but themselves," said Mel. "It's so nineties."

"What are you talking about?"

"You're blaming your Peter Pan complex on your mother."

"What Peter Pan complex?" Jack demanded.

"The one you're so proud of," she sniffed.

With a chuckle meant to convey disdain if not pity, Jack shook his head sadly. "Do you have any friends?"

"I don't have time for friends," Mel argued.

"That's because you have a Captain Hook complex," he announced triumphantly.

"A what?"

"A Captain Hook complex," he repeated.

Mel hiked her shoulder, adjusted the leather straps of her bag. "There's no such thing," she said.

"Yes there is and you have it," Jack insisted.

Mel whirled away from him. Then stopped, slipped her black bag off her shoulder, and pulled out his cellular. "Here's your phone back." She jabbed it into his big, puffed-up chest.

He grabbed it and plucked her phone from his belt. "And here's yours. Goodbye," he said.

"Goodbye," Mel repeated icily. She watched him turn and walk toward Amsterdam Avenue, and she shook her head. Then she set out quickly in the opposite direction, to Broadway, to pick up a new pair of stockings and catch the subway back down to Vincent's.

1:30 P.M.

City Hall was set in a small green park surrounded by magisterial courthouses and office towers. Around midday, the sun had speared through the clouds, lighting the diminutive building with an unearned benevolence. Across the fast-drying asphalt in front of City Hall, where pickets and protesters usually demonstrated, the park filled with people. Bureaucrats and bicycle messengers, lawyers and office workers, stock brokers and students lined up before hot dog vendors, falafel stalls, and pizza stands to grab a quick lunch in the sun. Newspapers were spread out on the still-wet benches. Couples formed. Frisbees appeared. Cigarettes were lit.

By one o'clock, pigeons and squirrels foraged in the grass, arrogantly appraising sandwich crusts, peanut shells, and pretzel ends. A Frisbee sailed over Jack's head as he ascended the subway steps.

"I swear, man, I'm just trying to get home to Jersey

and I lost my wallet," a spiky-haired youth with a
devil tattooed on the wrist of his outstretched arm
told Jack.

"Best of luck," Jack said. And hurried across the
park to City Hall. Inside the building, an officious
blue suit blocked the corridor leading to the Mayor's
office.

Jack flashed his press card.

"I know who you are," the skinny man said, smiling at Jack. "I'm Richard Dupres, Mr. Taylor. And
I'm sorry. The Mayor is occupied. As you may have
heard, he's preparing to speak at five this afternoon.
I'll be happy to supply you with a press release
then—with the full text of that speech."

"Listen, Dick," Jack said, "I don't want to see Aikens. I'm looking for Manny Feldstein. I heard he's
locked in there with His Honor."

Dupres' face shifted into neutral. "I'm sorry, Mr.
Taylor. Mr. Feldstein is indisposed today."

Jack made a sudden move to pass Dupres. He was
startled by the slim man's quick, reflexive block. Dupres' arms shot out and he positioned himself more
aggressively in Jack's path. "I said, he's indisposed,"
Dupres repeated.

"Is that right, Dick? Well I'm disposed to smack
people who use euphemisms like indisposed when
what they really mean is . . ." Jack raised his voice
and hollered past Dupres: "Manny Feldstein is being
held against his will by the Mayor's office!"

Behind the blue suit, a bathroom door opened and

a balding man, rubbing his hands together in a classic compulsive gesture of guilt, Jack thought, stepped out into the hall.

"Hey!" Jack yelled.

The man turned abruptly, took one look at him, and ran in the opposite direction.

"FELDSTEIN!" Jack bellowed, throwing his shoulder into Dupres and knocking the startled, slender suit aside. "Feldstein, you treacherous prick," he yelled, barging past Dupres and taking the stairs behind Manny two at a time. "Stop! It's me, Manny. Stop!"

Feldstein tore down the narrow corridor at the top of the stairs, heading straight for the open window at the end of the hall.

"Are you nuts, Manny? What, are you going to kill yourself? You going to jump out that window to avoid me?!"

The apparently terrified Comptroller scrambled through the open window onto a fire escape. Jack charged after him, climbing out and catching Manny's belt. He gripped it tightly. Manny grabbed the railing as if he thought Jack were planning to pry him loose and throw him over the edge.

"I'm sorry, Jack. Please don't hit me," he begged, cowering against the railing.

Jack let go of the belt and straightened up. "You think I'm going to hurt you? What's the matter with you? Do you know me or what? I'm not going to hit you, Manny. But goddammit!"

The chubby, balding man stood up and cautiously released the iron railing.

"This morning I had the scoop of the year, and now I'm about to lose exactly all of my credibility," Jack continued. "Manny, Manny—I watched you play Tevye in dinner theater. I danced with Ida. Don't do this to me, please. Stay on the record, Manny, like a good snitch."

Manny had begun to nod his head. Now he brushed off his tie and said proudly, but with a dangerous hint of nostalgia, "I was a good snitch, wasn't I, Jack?"

"Not was, Manny. You are. The best. Now what's going on?"

It took a moment. "I've been having second thoughts," Manny said.

"But we'd already decided. We were going to get these guys. These are bad guys," Jack reminded him. "What happened to the Manny who stood in my living room and said this garbage thing stinks? Those were brave thoughts."

"I've been having some trouble with the dosage on my medication," Manny said softly. "The thing is, you get the dosage wrong, you get a little grandiose. We were talking about taking down the mayor and the mob together, right?"

"Right," Jack said enthusiastically.

"But that's crazy," Manny pointed out.

"It's not."

"I'm telling you it is," Manny said sadly. "Now

that I'm a little more regulated I realize they would definitely kill me."

"Don't do this to me," Jack urged, seizing Manny's shiny lapels and shaking him. "Please don't do this to me. I was the one who started your standing ovation for 'If I Were a Rich Man'! Manny, don't hang me out to dry!"

Manny hung limply in Jack's grasp. "I can't do it, Jack. I've got a wife and family. I'm their guy too. You're hurting my neck."

Jack released his grip.

"Sorry, Jack," Manny said.

He gave up. "Alright. Okay." He tried to smile. "Forget about it, okay? I'll figure it out."

"Jack," Manny said softly, apologetically, "I just got cast in 'The Music Man.' I'm going to play Harold Hill. I'll try to get you comps."

Two uniformed security guards suddenly scrambled out onto the fire escape below them. They wasted no time rushing up, grabbing Manny, and hauling him down the metal fire-escape stairs back toward the Mayor's office. "Hey!" Jack shouted, as they brushed by him. "Leave him alone. Do you know who I am?"

A third guard appeared and seized Jack's arm. He was a huge, surprisingly agile man whose sausage fingers were nervously fondling his holstered service revolver. "Let's move it, buddy," he said, left hand clamping Jack's bicep like an inflated blood pressure band. "Let's go."

He roughly escorted Jack down to the street, then released him with a shove toward the park. Jack stumbled and turned. From the sidewalk, he looked back up and caught a glimpse of Manny's apologetic face just before he disappeared back inside the building.

"This isn't over yet, goddammit," he grumbled.

The big guard turned menacingly.

"Yeah, that's right. That's what I said," Jack repeated, rubbing his arm where the guard had held him. Adrenaline charged wildly through him. He could feel his heart pound. He heard a ringing in his ears.

It was the cellular. "You heard me," he sneered at the guard, unhooking the phone from his belt. "Excuse me, I gotta get this."

— Eight —

Melanie had caught an express train downtown to Vincent's loft. Now, heading back to her office by taxi, the usually impossible midday traffic seemed to be parting for her like the Red Sea for Charlton Heston. Her luck was finally turning, Mel thought, as she sat with the exquisite model in her lap, fully repaired.

Her cell phone rang. She pulled it out of her bag with one hand and clicked on. "Hello?"

"Mommy?" Sammy's voice was barely audible through his tears.

Mel's heart sank. "What happened?"

"I don't want to stay here anymore," he said. "And neither does Maggie."

He sounded so unhappy, so little and desperate. "But, sweetie," she said softly, "you have to stay there. Just for a little—" Suddenly she heard another small, tearful voice. "Sammy, who's crying? Who's there with you?"

"Maggie," he answered. "She doesn't want to stay here, too."

"Really? I've never heard Maggie cry before. What happened?" Mel asked, beginning to panic.

"Spider-Man kicked me . . ."

"Oh, sweetie—"

"And She-Ra took Maggie's snack," he added, an edge of outrage cutting through his misery.

"Let me talk to the teacher," Mel said crisply. The cab's progress had been diverted by a street-cleaning truck which had forced traffic into two suddenly clogged lanes. A cacophony of horns and shouts commenced. Her own driver joined the fray in a language Mel had never heard before, guttural and staccato at the same time. They were only a dozen blocks from the office.

"She's not here," said Sammy.

"Why not? Where is she?" Mel demanded.

"She's outside talking to the Hulk about not using the 'f' word."

Mel took a deep breath. "Sammy, you're just going to have to be brave and tough," she began, "and wait for me—"

"Hang on, Mom," Sammy said. She could hear him conferring with Maggie, who remarkably still seemed to be snuffling back tears. When he returned a second later, he said, "What's LSD?"

"What do you mean, 'What's LSD?' " Mel almost shouted.

"You know that stupid Spider-Man kid? He told Maggie he was going to make her eat LSD that he got from his brother—"

"Don't move!" Mel barked. "Stay right where you are, you and Maggie both. You'll both be picked up in ten minutes."

She leaned back against the lumpy leather back-seat, shut her eyes, and murmured a tiny prayer. Her eyes stung. Her chest was tight, rippling with waves of panic. Help, was the prayer. Jack, came the answer. No way, Mel thought, even as she punched his number into her phone.

"Hello?" Jack growled.

"Jack, it's Melanie Parker," she said. "We have a major problem with our kids. I mean, they're okay but— Er, where are you?"

"At the zoo," he replied angrily, glaring at the security guard who shrugged dismissively and clumped back toward the building. "City Hall," he explained. "Why, what's happening?"

"They can't stay at the day care center. They have to be picked up right now. Can you do it?"

From the sidewalk, Jack looked back up at the window where he'd last seen Manny Feldstein's contrite face. "Um . . ." he murmured. Manny was gone.

Mel took a deep breath. "It would definitely jeopardize my career and, by extension, my entire life if I pick them up now. How about if I watch them both during your press conference if you'll watch them both from now until say three or three-thirty?"

Jack exhaled luxuriously. "Excuse me? Are you asking me for help?"

She could hear his smile over the phone. "It would appear that way, wouldn't it?" She could not afford a display of indignation now, she reminded herself.

"This is so hard for you, isn't it?" he asked smugly.

She blew her hair out of her eyes and evaded the question. "Are you agreeing or not?" she said.

He actually chuckled: It was a soft, throaty, self-satisfied sound. "I'll agree," he crooned mischievously, "if you say, 'Jack, please be my Knight in Shining Armor.' "

"Jack, don't be a shithead," she said. "Go rescue our kids."

"You know, you're not the only one with a day," he reminded her, aggrieved suddenly. "I've got a day, too."

"Sorry. I'll meet you and the kids in the lobby of 345 Park Avenue at three-fifteen, okay?"

"Fine," said Jack, and hung up.

As Melanie clicked off her mobile phone, the cab pulled up before the Arts and Architecture Building. The sound of Jack Taylor's voice stayed with her and she could feel a smile creeping across her face. He was so . . . cute was the word that came to mind. Adorable. Such childish words. Well, Mel thought, not unkindly, he was a childish kind of guy really. She guessed this sudden benevolence toward him stemmed from the immense relief she felt. At least Sammy was safe—

"Nuts!" she blurted out and quickly redialed Jack's number.

"What?" he demanded.

"I forgot to tell you. Sammy's allergic to shellfish and animal dander. Also, he's not allowed to watch commercial TV and no matter what he says he has to hold your hand when he crosses the street. Also, if you go to the playground, I like to check the sandbox first. You never know what people throw in there."

"You are a piece of work," he said.

In the cab on the way up to 98th Street, Jack phoned Hal.

"You were right. They got to him. Manny's pretty much out of the picture," he said. "Help me here. Who else would know about the kickbacks?"

"Sorry," Hal commiserated. "The mayor's campaign manager," he suggested.

"Eddie McCoy never talks. How about the City Comptroller?"

"Who is not going to implicate himself," Hal pointed out.

Jack reached for the marble, rubbed it between his fingers. "Hey, hey, hey," he said with new enthusiasm. "Elliot Lieberman! The Sanitation Commissioner's got to know."

"Yup, only he's not even here. Lieberman's in Barbados with his girlfriend."

"I read that, I knew that," Jack said, disgusted. Then, he brightened again. "Which leaves his very angry wife."

"Yes, keemo-sabe," said Hal, chuckling.

A city bus was enveloping Jack's taxi in tailpipe fumes. The cab driver was shaking his head. "Pollution, filth! They never give them summonses. D'ja ever see a bus get pulled over? Never. Never in your life would you see that."

"Lieberman." Jack kissed his magic marble and put it away. "Hal, I've got to go deal with something. Think Celia can track down the home number for Elaine Lieberman?"

The cab lurched from behind the bus and carved itself a new lane. Determined to let the bus driver know about the ecological threat he was posing, Jack's cab driver put on a burst of speed.

"Any excuse to talk to Celia is okay with me," Hal said. "Certainly."

Jack looked out the taxi window. His name and face, two feet high and four feet wide, looked back at him from the side of the bus.

"No retraction today, my friend," he told Hal.

The big man laughed his wheezing laugh. "We'll see."

"And you know what? Lew's never going to fire me because my picture's on buses all over the city and I've got a lot of loyal readers," Jack said.

"Frank Burroughs is on buses too." said Hal jovially.

"Lew's never going to replace 'You Don't Know Jack' with 'Frankly Speaking.' Frank Burroughs is too highbrow for my readers."

"Yeah, but I hear he wants to get into the grittier stories. Change his image a little, you know?" Hal reported. "Supposedly he just started wearing a baseball cap."

"A Yankees cap?" Jack asked, worried now.

"What else?" said Hal.

"Damn."

In the ladies' room, Mel changed her pantyhose, then rinsed her face and hands. As she walked across to the towel dispenser, hands dripping in front of her, Evelyn entered the bathroom.

"Ah, Frankenstein's mother," she quipped, eyeing Mel's awkwardly outstretched arms. "Where's the little Terminator?"

"You've got your heroes mixed up," Mel said, drying her hands.

"You're telling me." Evelyn peeked under the stall doors. "If he's in here, you really ought to let people know. Post a warning notice."

"Evelyn," Mel said coolly, "I'm sorry if you were inconvenienced."

"Here." The receptionist handed Mel a Ninja Turtle. "It was in my shoe."

"Raphael," Mel murmured, studying the tiny figure.

"Donatello, I think," Evelyn corrected her. "I've

got a nephew. But don't let Leland know."

Mel tucked the toy into her bag and began repairing her makeup.

"So what'd you do, send him to his father?"

"He's with a friend," Mel said. "Well, with the friend of a friend, really. The ex-husband of a friend. Not really. I mean, she's not exactly a friend. A neighbor. Her daughter goes to school with Sammy."

"So you farmed him out to a stranger?"

Mel stared at Evelyn, startled. "Just kidding," the woman said. "At least he's a guy. They need guys, you know. Little guys need big guys. Hey, even I need guys. How about you?"

"What time is it?" Mel asked.

"If you want to know whether the Yates boys are here, the answer is yes. They stepped off the elevator about two minutes ago. And almost tripped on this." She pulled a purple Matchbox car out of her pocket.

Mel snatched the car and tossed it into her bag.

"Good luck," Evelyn called as Mel scurried out the door.

In the conference room, on Smith Leland's prized lacquered table, the shopping-mall model all but glistened under its spotlight. Mel stood behind it, alone, poised, fresh, alert, prepared. She checked the hallway, looked at her watch again, and decided she had time to make one quick call. Eyes on the conference room door, she pulled out her phone and dialed.

"Hello?" Jack Taylor answered.

"Hi, it's me," Mel said, unable to keep the gratitude out of her voice, or the smile from her lips.

"Me who?" Jack asked flirtatiously.

The automatic response, his coquettish knee-jerk reaction to an anonymous female voice, wiped away her smile. "Do you have the kids?" she asked, all business now.

"I sure do," Jack said pleasantly. "They're both fine. Hear that?" He held the phone away so that she could hear both children laughing hysterically. "Jack, Jack, Jack," Sammy gasped delightedly. "Daddy, stop," Maggie shrieked between giggles. He was tickling them. She was sure of it. She drummed her fingers on the conference table waiting for him to get back on the line. "I just picked them up. They're safe and sound. We're leaving the center now," he said.

"I just wanted to, er . . . well, to . . ."

"You just wanted to check up on me," he interrupted good-naturedly. "Because you don't really trust me, right? You only asked me to watch Sammy out of sheer desperation and part of you would feel safer with him at the Ninety-eighth Street Day Care Center dropping LSD with Spider-Man. Isn't that true?"

"No, that isn't true. I only wanted to warn you that Sammy can get into trouble faster than you can make most women smile."

"That fast?" he teased.

"Please just really pay attention to him."

"I won't let him out of my sight," Jack promised.

"Jack, can I have that?" she heard Sammy squeal.

"What?" she asked, thinking *Playboy* magazine, a miniature bottle of airline scotch, a little black book full of phone numbers, a condom . . . "What does he want?"

"My marble," Jack said, "I was just fooling around with it. Tell me something, Melanie," he asked. "What does it take to make *you* smile?"

She smiled. "Sammy safe in the lobby at three-fifteen," she said.

Jack didn't believe her. "I'm sure," he insisted, "it takes a lot more than that."

Mel clicked off and slipped her phone back inside her black bag. She'd barely had time to smooth back her hair when Leland entered with the two Yateses of Yates & Yates Development Company.

They were a father and son team, both big men in jaunty plaid jackets and bolo string ties. Melanie had met them briefly, only once before. Now she ransacked her memory for their names.

Carl and Joe, she thought. No, that wasn't it. Her palms began to sweat. She thrust them into her jacket pockets. She probably looked like a prosecuting attorney now, she decided. Nothing to do about it, but wet her lips and smile more broadly at them. Finally Leland said, "Kurt, Joseph, you remember Melanie Parker?"

Kurt. Kurt! Her momentary relief faded as she realized she didn't know which one of them was Kurt.

"Yes indeedy," the older man said, extending his hand.

As discreetly as possible, Melanie dried her palm and reached out to him.

"Mr. Yates," she nodded. "So good to see you. And . . ."

"Joseph," the younger man prompted.

"Of course," she seized his hand with fervent gratitude.

Their polite smiles vanished instantly as they turned to inspect the model. She'd put her all into designing an elegantly practical shopping center. Melanie glanced at Smith Leland. His welcoming grin was also gone. His lean, gray face had become a mirror of the Yateses concentration. Leland's eyebrows went up abruptly. Melanie turned back to the clients and, as she'd anticipated, saw that Kurt Yates' bushy black eyebrows had reared up as well.

What? What?! she felt like shouting. Then she saw a little grin reappear on Joseph's pursed lips. It spread to his father's face. The Yateses were smiling. *Yes!*

"I love it," Kurt decided. "It's simple and stylish."

Now that it was safe, Melanie felt the air whoosh out of her. She hadn't realized she'd been holding her breath. She allowed herself to smile, and a grateful little laugh burbled out of her. Leland pulled his Sulka handkerchief out of his breast pocket and daubed his brow. He met her eyes and nodded.

"All it needs now," Joseph added, "is a parking lot full of cars."

Mel reached into her black bag and grabbed a handful of Sammy's Matchbox cars which she set down one by one in the parking lot area of Vincent's wonderful model.

Kurt Yates laughed aloud. "This one's a real discovery," he said to Leland.

Patting Melanie's back with an enthusiasm usually reserved for clients, Leland said, "Yes she is."

She dipped her head modestly. "Thank you. I'm happy you—"

"I hope you'll be joining us for drinks later to celebrate," said the younger Yates.

"Let's say five-thirty at the 21 Club," his father concluded, once more extending a hand that looked to Mel like a calloused ham.

She took it. "Er . . ." she said. "I don't know if I can . . ."

"We won't take no for an answer," Yates Jr. added.

On her shoulder, Leland's congratulatory pat had turned into a vise-like grip.

Mel sighed. "I'll be there," she said.

2:30 P.M.

They'd gotten off the subway at Fifty-ninth and Broadway and walked east along the edge of the park. "Hey, isn't this great?" Jack asked enthusiastically. He slapped his chest and inhaled the fresh spring air. The billowy clouds had parted. The sun sparkled off wet leaves and grass and green wooden benches. Traffic whizzed by on Central Park South, tires shushing along the wide, damp pavement.

"See, you don't have to plan everything," he called to Sammy, who had worriedly asked, "Where are we gonna go now, Jack?" and "What're we gonna do?"

"You don't have to know what you're going to do every minute of the day," he'd explained, on the ride down.

"My mom likes to plan things," the little boy had replied. "She likes to be safe, not sorry."

"She's smart." Jack had ruffled his hair. "But you've got to leave room for chance, too," he'd said. "For magic. Sometimes, Sammy, the best things in the world happen—just like that!"

The kid had looked skeptical. Now there he was kicking a bottle cap down the street, carefree and happy as could be. Impulsively Jack reached into his pocket. "Sammy?" he called. "Do you still have my marble?"

The boy pulled it out of his pocket and waved it. "Can I still hold it, Jack?"

"Abso-Sammy-lutely," he called.

"Sammy is a showoff," Maggie said, squeezing her father's hand emphatically.

"He's okay, Maggs. For a boy," he teased her.

Every few minutes, Sammy would peer over his shoulder, and offer Jack a shy grin. And whenever the boy turned, Jack noticed, Maggie's grip on his own hand tightened. Whether she was jealously claiming him or her brief stint at the day care center had made her uncharacteristically insecure, he didn't know. It suited him fine, though, to feel his daughter's sturdy little grip.

"I'm not going to play any baby games with Sammy," she announced loudly.

"S'not a baby game," Sammy balked. "It's just like soccer. I'm practicing for later. And anyway, you're the baby."

"Hey, hey, hey," Jack said, slick as Solomon, "it's too nice a day to squabble-bobble, am I right or am I right?" The scent of wet asphalt mingled with the park's rich loam. "Smell that?" he said to his daughter. "Smell that?" he called to Sammy. Then he breathed in exaggeratedly, and picked up another heady scent.

"Eeeewww, Dad!" Maggie held her nose.

"Wow, horses!" said Sammy, taking off at a run for the line of carriages at the entrance to the park.

"What do you think, Maggie Magpie? Would you like to pet a horsey?"

Maggie nodded, released his hand, and took off after Sammy. By the time Jack reached them, they were giggling together and patting the neck of a horse who was busily plundering a feed bucket. "How much for half an hour?" he asked the driver.

"Forty-five," the young man said. He was wearing a checkered vest and battered top hat.

"Okay! Hop in gang," Jack told the ecstatic children.

"Oh, boy, Jack," Sammy said. "This is going to be great. And it just . . . happened! Like you said!"

"Stop talking to my Daddy," Maggie said crossly.

"Okay, let's all sit back and relax and go for a ride. Big smiles, now. Maggie-Waggie, where's my smile?"

She began to giggle. "Excellent, excellent," Jack said. "Excuse me for a moment now." He unhooked his mobile phone, dialed his office and asked for Celia's extension.

"Well, hiiii, Jack," she said.

"How'd you know it was me?" he asked.

"A girl can hope," said Celia. She gave him Elaine's home number.

"You're beautiful!"

"Yes," said Celia, "I know."

He clicked off and dialed immediately.

"Daddy?" Maggie tugged at his sleeve.

Jack put a quieting finger to his lips. "Elaine Lieberman please—"

"Da-ad," she sang impatiently.

"*No puedo*," said the person who answered the phone. "Mrs. Lieberman *no esta a la casa*."

"Wait," Jack told Maggie, then into the phone again, talking fast, he implored, "Look, it's very important. Couldn't you *try* to speak English?"

Maggie was waiting.

"Don't hang up! *Por favor, por favor . . .*"

Lieberman's maid hung up.

Jack swore into the dialtone. He clicked off and hooked the phone back on his belt. "Okay, what're we going to do next, huh?" he said, rubbing his hands together.

"Jack, why do you call someone who can't speak English a ship?" Sammy asked.

"Hey, what's that over there?" Jack said enthusiastically. The Museum of Natural History's dinosaur flag was flying. And there was another exhibit, something about amber. "How about that?" He pointed to the flags. "Want to go see the dinosaurs?"

"Yes, yes, yes!" Maggie shouted.

"Okay," said Sammy, carefully tossing Jack's marble in the air and catching it with two hands.

Maggie gave him a nasty look. "It's not even yours," she said.

Jack asked the carriage driver to drop them at Tavern on the Green. From there, they walked west to the museum.

He turned them loose on the dinosaur floor, then started making calls. "Burton Monash's office, please," he said. "Yes, hi, this is Jack Taylor, *Newsday*. I wondered if you could tell me if Mr. Monash is representing Elaine Lieberman in her divorce? No? Thank you."

He dialed information and got Raul Feldar's number, then decided to check in at his office again.

"Hal? Anything? Anything at all? I just spoke to—"

"Jack?" Hal interrupted him. "Hang on there, panty man. I got nothing new, but Celia wants you. I'm going to transfer you."

"I don't have time for Celia now, Hal."

"No, no. She's got something on Lieberman, I

think." The big man did his wheezing chuckle. "What a babe," he said, "Hang on."

"Jaa-ack." Celia's seductive opening irritated him.

"Whatcha got?" he said abruptly.

"Oooo, so masterful. Okay, here's the deal. I was just about to call you. Elaine is suing for divorce."

"I had a hunch," he said. "Did you get her lawyer's name? I tried Monash and I was just about to dial Feldar. I need to get to her fast."

"Her maid said she does volunteer work at a local hospital," Celia offered.

"You speak Spanish?" Jack was impressed.

"Aren't I full of surprises?" she crooned.

He reached into his inside pocket and pulled out his notepad and pen. "Which hospital? Shoot."

"I'm good but not that good, Jack. Carlita didn't know. Want me to call around?"

"Daddy?"

"What?" Jack said sharply. He saw Maggie flinch slightly. "Oh, gosh. I'm sorry Maggie Magpie. Celia," he said, "I've got to go. Call me if you get anything else."

"Will do," she said, and he hung up.

"Sorry, Maggs. Didn't mean to grumble-bumble. I'm not mad at you at all. I'm just ... Hey, never mind. What's up? Are we having fun yet?"

She giggled and nodded yes. "Can we go to the planetarium? Please?"

"Is that all?" Jack teased.

"Yeah, can we?" Sammy chimed in.

"The planetarium?!" He was grinning at them again. His voice sing-songing just like theirs. "Boy, that sounds like fun . . . But we don't even really have time for *this*. Sammy, my man, your mom will kill me if I don't have you in her lobby by three-fifteen on the dot."

"I don't think she'd kill you," Sammy replied earnestly. "She's not like that really."

"She isn't?" He put a hand on each of their shoulders and led them toward the exit.

"No," Sammy said, blinking up at him. "She'd just rather be safe than sorry."

Jack laughed. "And what does that mean?"

Sammy smiled shyly and shrugged. "She says it a lot when, you know, guys try to open her door and call her stupid and stuff." He reached into his pocket and brought out Jack's marble, and began to roll it around in his hand.

"Quit trying to be like my Dad," Maggie hissed at him.

"Am not," Sammy whispered back.

"Are so," her voice got louder.

"Am *not*!" Sammy shouted.

"So, Sammy," Jack interrupted as they started down the broad marble staircase. "Tell me something, how long have your mom and dad been divorced?"

"I don't know." Sammy shrugged. "But my Dad's coming to my soccer game today. Probably."

"So you see your dad a lot?"

"Pretty much," Sammy said proudly, rolling the marble on his palm. "Usually. He has a different schedule than other daddies. My dad's a drummer. But his favorite thing to do is watch me play soccer."

"Hah!" said Maggie.

Sammy ignored her. "He is definitely probably coming today," he said. "And he's taking me fishing this whole summer. Just us. And maybe mommy will come, too."

Maggie was looking at them suspiciously, her wide eyes moving from one to the other.

"Wow, a drummer," Jack said sincerely. "He sounds like a really great guy, Sammy."

Maggie couldn't stand it anymore. "Give me that," she said, grabbing the marble.

"He gave it to *me*!" Sammy shouted. In a flash, he'd grabbed it back, surprising Maggie. Even Jack was impressed with his sudden aggressive agility.

"Hey, hey, hey, you guys," Jack said, trying to mediate. He put his hands between them. "Take turns, okay?"

Sammy clung stubbornly to the marble as Maggie tried to pry open his hand.

— Nine —

The WNYC weather and traffic helicopter swooped low over the city. Both levels of the George Washington Bridge, George and Martha, it reported, were moving freely. The Henry Hudson Parkway looked pretty good, too, until you got down around the boat basin, where a fallen tree branch had begun to cause a bottleneck. Under the thunderous thumping rotary beat, the chopper banked east and headed toward Central Park. The 86th Street transverse was flooded again. Yellow police sawhorses blocked the roadway, causing traffic on Central Park West to start backing up in both directions. A couple of motorists had gotten out of a car and a van, respectively, and were mixing it up near the 65th Street entrance to the park.

The East Side was, as usual, orderly and slow moving. A yellow sea of taxis, parted intermittently by white and green buses and the occasional hemmed-in car, clogged upper Fifth Avenue. The Metropolitan Museum's massive flags dwarfed the traffic, and, here and there on terraces and rooftops, genteel gardens mirrored in miniature the park's verdant landscape.

"Mary! Please close the terrace doors," Liza McKenna Wilson shouted. "What is that, an earthquake? Oh, God, hold on, Mel, please. I've got to go see what's going on. I can't hear myself think."

Sitting at the drafting table in her office, wolfing down the tuna on rye she'd fixed for herself last night, Mel waited with the phone crooked in her neck. Through her open door, she could hear Leland escorting the Messrs. Yates toward the elevator.

"Save some room for the steak tartare!" Kurt's happy moon face appeared at her door.

Quickly, Mel wiped away the blob of mayonnaise and tuna caught at the corner of her lip, and returned his manic grin.

"Oh, God," she groaned, when Liza returned from terrace inspection.

"There was a helicopter outside. What next?!" said her irate sister.

"Liza, I don't suppose you or anyone you know could watch Sammy and this guy's daughter for me from five-fifteen to five forty-five today?" There was no response. "I didn't think so," Mel rushed on. "Anyway, I'm really sorry about this morning. I didn't mean to imply that you don't do anything."

"No one could imply that," Liza said. Wrapped in the antique silk kimono Davis had brought home from his last trip to Japan, she was sitting at her dressing table holding alternate earrings alongside her face. "I just decorated six dozen clown cookies with four colors of frosting, sold them to three dozen sugar-crazed kids, and raised twenty-six dollars for Kyle's Fun Run."

With a sigh, she deposited the earrings back into the little porcelain bowl beside the silver-framed portrait of her children. "Of course, you *could* imply that I don't do anything *interesting*," she added.

Mel crumpled the Baggie in which her sandwich had been wrapped and hurled it at the wastebasket. There was not enough heft to it. It floated leisurely to the floor. "Well, but it's definitely worthwhile," she said, trying to cheer her sister.

"Right." Liza refused to be consoled. "I would have much rather just written him a check for twenty-six dollars and gone to a movie." She eyed the wooden florentined gold box on the Queen Anne table next to her chaise longue. There was a pack of cigarettes in it. It had been there since she'd quit smoking again, four weeks ago. Five maybe. Since then, she'd only snitched one from the pack. Surely another couldn't hurt.

"I swear, the pressure of being a stay-at-home mom is going to drive me back to work," she told Mel. "So how's your day?"

"Never-ending," Mel responded. And you chose it,

heckled the little critic in her head. Immediately, an anxious knot tightened in her gut. Maybe the mayo had gone rancid. Maybe she'd gulped down her sandwich too fast. Definitely she could have done without the coffee. Mel stared balefully at the paper *I Love NY* container which held the dregs of her burnt deli coffee. "I next have to somehow finesse drinks at Grand Central at five-thirty, which is the exact same time I'm supposed to be watching Sammy and this guy's daughter," she said to Liza.

"This guy?"

"Then there's Sammy's championship Pre-Little League soccer game," Mel hurried on. "In Central Park at six if it doesn't rain."

"That should be fun," Liza said distractedly.

"Except that I can't bear to see Sammy's face when his dad doesn't show up for his game again."

Liza carried her cordless over to the chaise. "I still don't know how you could have married that loser," she said. Her hand reached for the box lid and paused in mid-air.

"Losers are harder to recognize when you're nine-teen," Mel said.

Liza spun away from temptation and carried the phone toward her walk-in closets. "Mel," she asked suddenly. "Do you miss daddy?"

It took her a moment to switch gears, to hear the question. The answer was yes. The answer was so yes that the knot in Mel's gut gave a final wrench, then exploded. And tears sprang to her eyes. "Yeah, I guess," she said thickly.

"Me, too," said Liza. "They don't make men like that anymore, do they?"

The question, a statement really, surprised Melanie. Not that she hadn't thought it herself, and frequently. But Liza had Davis, Mel had always reasoned, faithful, generous, reliable, bestower of bird-kisses Davis. After a moment, Mel said, "He was one of the good guys, wasn't he?" He'd been a writer, her father, a scholar; well, a teacher, really. He'd written books on the Renaissance, slender, erudite works which had been published by the college where he taught art history. But he'd also written "books" especially for Mel and Liza. Clever fairy tales in which they were the characters, illustrated with his own funny line drawings, which he'd encouraged them to color in.

He was a tickler, her father, and a laugher and a great storyteller. Mel remembered their mother constantly swatting his hands away, laughing till tears ran down her cheeks, till she lost her breath and her patience and once whacked him with a wooden spoon so hard to make him stop that everyone in the kitchen—Mel coloring at the table; Liza on the linoleum floor, cutting out clothes for her paper doll; her father in his gray sweater which was beginning to unravel at one elbow; and her mother, Rita—was breathless and stunned. Everyone stopped. Everything.

"You hit me?!" her father had said, hurt, confused. And the three women all began to cry at once. What wailing! And Mel remembered, her dad had rushed from one to the other of them, making happy faces and smiling crazily, saying, "Hey, it's alright. I'm alright. I was just faking."

When he'd told them about the cancer, it was the same. Her mother, who had known for months, began to cry. And Mel and Liza had burst into tears, too. And there he'd been. His already thinning hair looking patchier than ever because of the chemotherapy, she'd realized later. His face gaunt, gray. And he'd run from one to the other of them again, trying to cheer them, saying everything would be alright, really. And then he'd sat down finally and let them rush to him and hold him, and they'd all cried together.

"He loved you best," Liza said now, matter-of-factly.

"Well," said Mel, unconsciously mimicking her father's self-deprecating humor, "it's a dirty job, but somebody had to do it."

"I guess," Liza responded mindlessly. "Oh, God, what am I going to wear . . . and why do I even care? I've got a million gorgeous evening dresses here. Some of them still have tags hanging on them. This damned dinner party is sending me over the edge. Sweetie, I'm sorry I can't help you today."

"Hey, it's all right." Mel found herself smiling consolingly, suddenly, crazily, wanting to comfort Liza.

"So I hear you might finally be dating again?" her sister said.

"What?!"

"Mom tells me you've got something going with some journalist."

"Hah!" Mel said, finishing the cold bitter coffee in a swallow, and hurling the cup into the wastepaper basket. "I just met him this morning," she protested. "He's irresponsible, self-absorbed, childish—"

"But cute, right?" Liza said slyly.

"Liza, what are you smoking?" Mel said, shaking her head.

"I am not smoking! I haven't had a cigarette in nearly forty-two goddamn days! And I'm doing an important dinner party tonight. And I am still not smoking! Do you have any idea how hard it is for me?"

"Not really," said Mel.

"How callous," Liza fumed.

"I meant, cute," Mel quickly amended. "You asked me if Jack Taylor was cute, didn't you? And I said, 'Not really.'"

She thought of his girl-killer grin, the wide shoulders on which he'd carried his daughter, that silly marble he rolled around his palms. A quiet warmth swirled in the emptiness the knot had opened in her gut. It warmed Mel, even made her smile.

"I mean, he is cute," she explained to her sister, laughing suddenly. "But not that cute."

3:00 P.M.

Jack's marble was stuck in Sammy's nose.

A horde of noisy students from John Jay College swarmed out onto the side street, crossing between the cars, cabs, and double-parked ambulances discharging passengers in front of St. Luke's. Street noises rang though the emergency room.

Each time a siren sounded, Sammy's head ratcheted longingly toward the window. But he couldn't see much. He was sitting on the high white examination table, swinging his feet back and forth, waiting for the emergency-room pediatrician to return.

Across the small white-curtained room, Jack was weighing himself. Maggie sat on a molded plastic chair staring at Sammy with disgust.

"You are so stupid," she said.

"Am not," Sammy grumbled. It was hard to understand him. *Ham nah* was what it sounded like he'd said.

"Are so!" Maggie insisted, leaping out of her chair, her little hands balled into fists at her side. "And you sound really stupid. And you look really, really stupid!"

It was true. With the marble stuck up his nose, wedged firmly in his nostril, half of Sammy's tear-stained face was grotesquely enlarged. "You're stupid. I'm smart," he insisted. "That's why Mrs. Fineman gave *me* the class fish to watch."

Maggie understood him perfectly. She drew closer

to the examination table. "You ruined my dad's marble," she countered. "He's not going to want it with your snot all over it."

"Sure I will." Jack stepped off the scale. "I'll just wash it off."

Humiliated, Sammy lowered his head. Tears started to run down his cheeks.

"Hey, come on, you're going to be alright." Jack lifted the boy's chin. "The doctor's just going to pop it right out of there."

"How come you couldn't pop it right out?" Sammy asked.

"Hey, little nose, *big* marble. But I bet the doctor'll have a special tool for just this kind of thing. It's going to be okay." Jack rubbed his hands together. "Let's see if we can't get your mind off your nose for a minute."

A football crashed into the metal grill covering the window. Sammy and Maggie whirled toward the sound. "It's nothing. Just kids outside," Jack assured them.

They were jumpy, he realized. And why wouldn't they be, sitting around in an emergency room waiting for a doctor? Sitting around in an overly air-conditioned sterilized space sucking up disinfectant fumes with nothing to distract them but the groaning next door and the chirp and rattle of gurneys being wheeled along the hallway.

They were such little guys, too, Jack thought, looking from one small, solemn face to the other. Well, not such a small face in Sammy's case. He could kick himself. She'd warned him not to leave the kid alone, hadn't she? Just the thought of Mel sent a shudder through him now, the thought of her Valkyrie rage, sword and breastplate, swooping down on him.

Okay, this was no time for recriminations, he told himself. Even Sammy's wise and perfect mommy, he felt sure, would agree. He'd been a pretty fair storyteller at Camp Conestoga, wowed them round the campfire and in the moonlit cabin after lights out.

Jack moved to the edge of his Howard Johnson's green hospital seat and cracked his knuckles. "Okay, listen up." He winked at Sammy, and drew Maggie closer. "So, you're in Mrs. Fineman's class. Is that her name?"

They nodded silently, mouths already slack, instantly signed up for the event.

"Okay, so it's a regular day, right? Kids are coloring, playing with blocks, hitting each other . . ." He play-acted childish hitting. It was a boffo success.

"Daddy!" Maggie giggled.

Sammy laughed, then winced and grabbed his nose.

"So out of the corner of your eye," Jack hurried on, "you notice the class bully . . ."

"Ralph Pugg," Maggie shrieked.

"Yeah, Ralph, Ralph," Sammy agreed.

"Ralph Pugg, exactly. He's pouring ink from Mrs.

Fineman's pen into the fishbowl. The fish are chok-ing, they're trying to get out. It looks like they're not going to make it."

Jack stood up and began to pace between them. "You scoop them up," he said to Sammy. "You change their water, give them fresh food—" He whirled toward Maggie. "And turn Ralph Pugg in. Pugg gets sent to the headmaster's office and they throw a party for the two of you!"

"Nnn-yes!" Sammy's little fist shot up.

"They give you unlimited Coke instead of juice. The whole school knows your name. Hi Maggie! Hi Sammy! People you don't even know start sending you Barbies and Ninja Turtles. You get a letter from Shari Lewis. Truckloads of Snickers and Cheese Doo-dles arrive. You don't even have to raise your hand to speak anymore because . . ." He drew it out in a conspiratorial whisper. " . . . when you open your mouth everyone else in the room just shuts right up, including Mrs. Fineman."

Straightening abruptly, he added, "*That's* the Pu-litzer Prize."

The curtain swung back with rapid efficiency. A big blond man in green surgical scrubs entered, ex-tending his hand to Jack. "I'm Dr. Weissman. So where's our nose problem?"

Sammy's eyes were riveted to the doctor's other hand, which was latex-gloved and wielding a gleam-ing pair of surgical pliers.

· 3:14 P.M.

In the lobby of the Arts and Architecture Building, Melanie tapped her toe and toyed with her beaded necklace. After pacing restlessly for some minutes, she had situated herself between the newly installed but not yet manned—or womaned—reception booth and the lobby's tubular steel planter. Although she loved flowers, Mel had always found the planter unattractive, sterile. And now some creative type, she noticed, had torn out last month's basic geraniums and ivy. The metal planter was currently crawling with strange drooping succulents; fat, pale plant fingers that seemed capable of producing pod people in the night.

Mel had come down to the lobby early. She'd been driven by one of the endless disaster scenarios she felt compelled to imagine and prevent. This one started with the idea that Jack Taylor might want to drop off the children before the agreed upon time. If he didn't find her waiting in the lobby, of course, he would bring them upstairs . . . where Leland would develop hives and, after stepping on an X-Man or a handful of colored pens, Yateses would fly . . . The possibilities were endless and terrifying. Mel hadn't taken the time to fully develop them. She'd grabbed her shoulder bag and headed for the elevator bank half expecting to bump into Sammy in the hall.

Now, of course, it was obvious that they were going to be late. Which would give her plenty of time to dream up an anthology of new disasters. Impatient, annoyed with herself, she checked the revolving door again, then glanced at her watch. "Typical," she muttered.

What a day. She was bone-weary, worn out by worry as much as the day's actual manic events. Mel yawned, and as she did, her cell phone rang. She fumbled it out of her bag and, still yawning, answered, "Hello?"

"Hey, sexy," a seductive female voice purred. "I miss you."

That woke her up. "I don't think so," Mel said. "Look, whoever you are, this isn't Jack's phone anymore. Er . . . who are you?" she added after a beat.

"Who are *you*?" the woman responded with curt curiosity.

"No," said Mel, "who are you?"

"This is Celia Leonard," Celia capitulated with a smug chuckle. "I'm a *friend* of Jack's. Who's this?"

"Absolutely nobody," Mel confessed.

"Oh." The information seemed to please Celia. At least it allowed her to get to the point. "Well, can you please tell Jack that his ex-wife just called from the Bahamas to let him know her number there? And also that Elaine Lieberman is at the Elizabeth Arden Salon until three-thirty today."

They were running as fast as they could. They were dashing down Park Avenue South dodging pedestrians and book peddlers, messengers with huge canvas bags slung across their shoulders, umbrella-topped fruit stands, incense sellers, metal tables piled with Gucci sweatshirts and Calvin Klein socks, dogs and dog walkers.

"How much time?!" Maggie shouted, delighted with the game.

She was fresh as a daisy. She wasn't even panting. "One minute." Jack tapped his thinning breath reserve to answer his remarkable daughter.

"Oh, no. Hurry!" Sammy urged them on.

"Boy, is your mom going to hate me," Jack called, "when she finds out you had to go to the emergency room!"

"No she won't. It wasn't the first time!" Sammy hollered cheerfully, tightening his grip on Jack's right hand. "I had to go for Grandma's wedding ring, too!"

The building was in sight. "Just the same, let's not tell her about this, okay?!"

"Okay!" Sammy was his man.

Maggie tugged at his left hand. "She's still gonna be mad at you, Daddy," she asserted.

"Why?!"

"Well I didn't want to say anything before," Maggie shouted, "because of your story, but Lois ate the class fish!"

"What?!" Sammy was horrified.

Jack swept him along, kept him moving. It took him a moment to understand what Maggie was talking about. Probably because he was running low on oxygen. He was still working on Lois. Lois? "Lois Lane! The cat?!" he wheezed. Bad idea. He should have saved the breath. He was sure he'd need it once they were inside the building.

Maggie leaned forward, at full speed, to taunt Sammy. "Boy, is Mrs. Fineman going to be mad at you," she told the shocked boy.

They were at the revolving door. "We'll buy more fish later," Jack gasped. He patted Sammy's skinny shoulders, then ran a hand over the boy's wild curls. He wanted to say something comforting, something buddy-like, light and breezy, but he had a stitch in his side and it was all he could do to breathe now.

They charged into the revolving door. And, as planned, exited walking slow and proud.

God, she looked good. Her face lit up at the sight of them. Those eyes just drank them in. All of them. Even him.

"Hi you guys!" she said. Then turning her smile and pale eyes full-strength on him—and notice, no diminution of smile here; no dimming of wattage whatsoever—she said, "Thanks so much for watching Sammy. Really. You saved my life."

Jack couldn't say anything. He had no breath left. He didn't want her to know that they'd worked up a sweat tearing through the streets of New York trying to avoid her wrath. Therefore, instead of trying to speak, he chose to nod and smile ingratiatingly at her.

She wasn't going to make it easy.

"Was he any trouble?" Mel asked.

Jack shook his head, put up a protesting palm,

waved away the very suggestion of difficulty. No trouble at all, was his mimed message.

"Good," Mel said. "So everything worked out great." Then she added, with a little lighthearted twinkle, "I was starting to think you were going to either show up three hours late or not at all."

He was not amused. Looking over the day, thinking about everything he'd been through, from Kristin's wakeup lecture and Lew Wilder's diatribe to Feldstein's defection and Sammy's emergency-room visit, he was not up for cute little jibes and jabs just now. Gasping for air, he drew himself up. "Guess what?" he sputtered, with what little dignity he could muster. "I'm not like every other man you know."

"I realize that," she said quickly, her green eyes sparking nervously. "I was just kidding."

"No you weren't," Jack said.

"Guess what?" she said, "I'm not like every other woman you know."

She looked like her kid when she said it. Am so, Am not, Are too. She was doing that little defensive thing Sammy did when Maggie got under his skin—chin hesitantly assertive, eyes uncertain. "Really?" Jack said, softening just a little, letting his guard down.

"Yeah," she rushed on. "You probably think I'm a real control freak—"

It had occurred to him.

"But I'm not at all. I mean I do like things the way

I like them, but who doesn't?" She didn't pause. She was not looking for an answer here. "And anyway, in my life, I'm the only one who does everything, so what does it matter?"

"Maybe you should let somebody help you once in a while," he reasoned.

"Are you saying that I behave as though I don't want or need help? That's ridiculous. Did you ever see the juggler outside the Met? You know, the tall skinny guy. Oh, sometimes he works outside Second Stage up on Broadway if there's a kids' show playing. Well, that's me. I'm, you know. I've got all these little balls up in the air. If somebody else caught one for me, I'd drop them all." She snorted. It was supposed to be an ironic little laugh, he guessed.

"And you're not a control freak?" he said.

Another snort, a bit testy this time. "No, I'm a single working mother," she announced.

"Well, I've got more work to do than time to do it in," Jack said, glancing purposefully at his watch. "So before we get into yet another lengthy and exhausting 'thing,' I've got an R-train to catch."

"Do you have any instructions for me before you go?" she asked coolly.

He said, "No. I trust you completely."

"Er . . ." she said. "Um . . . could you . . ."

He waited with a false and he hoped annoying smile.

"I don't suppose you could switch your thing from

five to four-thirty because I just found out that I have a new thing at five-thirty."

This was her idea of asking for help. "I can't switch my thing," he said.

She shrugged her slender shoulders. "I'll switch mine. No problem."

He gave her a curt nod, then bent down to kiss Maggie. "I'll see you at your soccer game," he said. Standing, he fished out his marble and tossed it in the air with a wink at Sammy. "See ya, buddy."

"By the way," Mel said, just as he was about to leave. "Your *friend* Celia called to tell you that Kristin called you from the Bahamas and also that somebody named Elaine Lieberman is at Elizabeth Arden's until three-thirty."

"Yeah, it's Spring Spa Day there," he said distractedly.

"You amaze me, Jack," Mel said.

He was about to nod again, to leave, when he was suddenly caught by her spectacular face. "Thank you, um . . ."

"Mel," she said, sarcastically. "I realize it's difficult what with Celia, Kristin, and Elaine and all, but—"

He watched her lips move. Beautiful. Her eyes flashing. He saw her do that pony toss with her hair again. "I know your name," Jack said quietly, savoring the word: "Mel."

He stared at her for a moment more, then left.

— Ten —

They were incredibly lucky, Melanie thought. They'd gotten a table at Serendipity about five minutes before a crowd of surburban matrons invaded the restaurant fanning themselves with *Playbills* and laughing about fallen gall bladders and sore feet. The restaurant, famous for its elaborate ice cream concoctions, was cozy, narrow and, for a weekday afternoon, much busier than Mel had imagined.

A busload of chic German tourists sat behind Sammy examining street maps and smacking their lips over immense sundaes. Alongside Maggie, an Italian-speaking family, blond, sun-tanned, burdened with enormous Bloomingdale's shopping bags, studied their colorful menus, chatting and gesturing elegantly.

"Now, Sammy, this is a special treat to make up

for everything bad that happened today." Mel guiltily explained away their presence in this rich and frivolous sugar-saturated world. "But you usually eat fructose instead of sugar so, when your ice cream comes, don't feel you have to finish the whole thing."

Flanked by the children, the back of Mel's chair rested an inch from the wall which was decorated with whimsical antique art, posters, and children's toys. "So," she said, "what did you guys do with Jack?"

A young waiter carrying three towering sundaes stopped at their table. "Okay, who's got the Forbidden Broadway and who's the Outrageous Banana Split?"

"We've all got everything," Melanie explained. "Just put them wherever."

"Wow!" said Sammy.

"I want the frozen hot chocolate," Maggie decided. Melanie switched her icy confection for Maggie's gorgeous gooey sundae.

Sammy dug into an enormous mound of whipped cream. "Jack took us on a horse-and-carriage ride," he said.

"Wow. That sounds like fun." Mel picked at her ice cream. It was amazingly delicious. "What else did you do?"

Unconsciously, Sammy touched his nose. Maggie kicked him under the table. "Nothing," Maggie said fiercely.

"Really?"

"Yeah. Nothing." Sammy nodded reassuringly at

Maggie. "We wanted to go to the planetarium, but Jack said we wouldn't have time. He wanted to rush back to you."

Maggie started to giggle. "Yeah, he made us run so fast!"

Now Sammy was giggling, too. "We were almost late, too."

Maggie kicked him again just as Mel looked up.

"Quit kicking me, Maggie. I wasn't going to say anything about—" He pointed to his nose.

There was a spot of whipped cream on the tip of it, Mel noticed. She wiped it for him. "About what?" she asked.

All of a sudden the two of them were laughing again. It was infectious. Mel smiled, too. She looking quizzically from one happy child to the other. They were giggling like little conspirators.

"What?" she asked, laughing with them.

"Nothing," Sammy said.

"It's a secret," Maggie explained. "We're not supposed to say."

Mel scooped up a big spoonful of ice cream, banana, and syrup. "About what?" she asked, holding it inches from her mouth. "About your Dad?"

Maggie nodded yes.

Mel quickly cleaned the dripping spoonful. "Mmmm," she said, eyelids fluttering with ecstasy.

"And about you too, Mommy," Sammy said.

She opened her eyes. "Really? About me?"

The children burst into giggles again.

"About me, too? Come on, you two. Tell."

Sammy and Maggie shook their heads and continued giggling. Mel couldn't help smiling, too. A secret about Jack and her, she mused. What could it be?

She thought about the look he'd given her just before he'd left the lobby. To tell the truth, she'd been thinking about it. She remembered how Jack had pronounced her name—and yes, it had sent very nice shivers through her.

I know your name, Mel. Her name, sweeter in his mouth than the extraordinarily wonderful sundae she was eating; warmer, too. And just as likely to give her a headache later on, Mel laughed. Had Jack actually said something to the kids about his feelings for her? Romantic feelings? Not that she minded, really. Jack Taylor was a terribly attractive man. And he had helped her out today. No doubt about it. She owed him.

Of course, it was totally inappropriate of him to confide in the children, to force a secret on them that they couldn't possibly keep. "A secret about me and Jack," she said now, good-naturedly. "Hmmm. Does it have to do with feelings?"

"What do you mean?" Sammy asked.

"You know. Feelings. Being scared or hurt, or being happy and excited. Those are all feelings."

Sammy was touching his nose again. "It *definitely* has to do with feelings, then." He looked at Maggie for confirmation.

"Yeah. Definitely," she agreed, and burst into giggles again.

"Okay, switch," Mel ordered, hands on her sundae dish. Following her example, they each passed their ice cream bowls to the person on their right.

"Mmmmm, what did you get?" Mel asked Maggie. "This is so good."

"Frozen hot chocolate."

"Yum," said Mel.

"You like chocolate?" Maggie asked, licking the syrup off her Forbidden Broadway spoon.

"I love chocolate," Mel confessed.

"Daddy told Dr. Martin this morning that he's got deep dark chocolate inside of him."

"Really?" Mel cocked her head at the little girl.

"And that he'd like to meet a fish who wasn't afraid of his dark chocolate layer."

"A fish? He said, a fish?"

Maggie nodded, unconcerned.

Mel began to smile again, and then to laugh. "I think I'm beginning to guess this secret," she said.

"Are you mad?" Sammy asked, instantly worried.

"Not really," Mel said. "I do think he should have talked about it with me, though."

Maggie looked up from her sundae. "He was afraid you'd hate him," she explained.

Mel reached over and wiped the little girl's chin. "Of course, I wouldn't hate him," she assured the child. "Honestly, that is so silly."

*   *   *

By the time they finished their ice cream and took turns going to the bathroom, there was a line at the cashier's counter. In fact, the entire front area of the store was crowded and bustling. Tourists, with and without children in tow, milled around displays that contained everything from Limoges boxes, books, and toys, to Etch-a-Sketch watches, flashing rings, and a device that spun lollypops for decadently quicker licking.

Mel stood on line with her credit card at the ready. Sammy had wandered over to the novelty shelf and was examining a box full of miniature pink babies. She peered between the shifting bodies of a family crowded near the door. A little tiger-striped kitten had wandered into the store and they moved to let it pass. It made directly for Maggie and was delightedly rubbing against her legs.

The woman at the head of the line was depositing an arm-load of toys and books on the counter. Mel shifted her feet and glanced at her watch. She had plenty of time. Jack's press conference wasn't until five. And shortly after that, when she failed to appear at the Yateses' command performance at 21, she'd be out of a job and have all the time in the world.

Such thoughts did not mix well with the sugar overdose she'd just ingested. Her stomach lurched. She stood on tiptoes, then crouched down to wave at Maggie, who was now sitting on the floor next to an umbrella stand playing with the kitten. Mel had just spotted Sammy, dancing two pink babies across a counter top, when her phone rang.

The only people who didn't turn to look at her as she foraged in her bag for the cellular were the ones checking to make sure their phones weren't ringing. "Hello?" Mel said, wondering if it might be Jack.

"Well, don't you sound chipper?" Her perpetually enthusiastic mother sounded pleased. "Hi darling."

"Mom. Thank God it's you. I'm in such big trouble. I have to have drinks with clients at five-thirty or I'll be fired, and I have absolutely no child care."

One of the *Playbill* ladies was listening, shaking her head with a look of disconcerting compassion.

Mel began to whisper. "When are you done at Elizabeth Arden?" Sammy had forsaken his babies and was now peering into a pricey little Limoges dish. "Sammy put that down," Mel hissed. "You'll break it."

"Melanie, you know how I admire your talent, dear," her mother was saying. "You're an absolutely brilliant young architect and your father was—and *is*, I'm sure—very, very proud of you. But your career . . . your job, I mean. It can't be the only thing you ever think about, darling. There's so much more to life—"

"I do not only think about work, Mom. I am thinking about my personal life. Actually, today I did. I thought about my personal life today."

Mel ducked down and searched through the thicket of adult legs for Maggie. She was no longer near the umbrella rack. She found the little tiger-striped cat first; it was licking its paws under a counter near the door.

"Excuse me," a man behind Mel said, indicating that the line was creeping forward.

"Of course," Mel said, stepping up to fill the six inches of vacated space before her. Still clutching her credit card and the bill, she listened to Rita and rolled her eyes. "You sound like you know him better than I do," she finally broke in. "What do you mean, don't be my usual self with him, Mom? My usual self couldn't be that bad because I'm pretty sure Jack just told the kids that he has feelings for me and that he wants to ask me out on a date."

Rita was delighted. But then Rita was delighted with facials and her new dentist and the program at the Roundabout this season. "Maggie?" Mel called. "Sammy, where's Maggie?"

Sammy had returned to the little rubber babies and was putting one up his nose.

"Take that thing out of your nose!" Mel growled hoarsely. "What's the matter with you? Mom," she said, when Sammy had sullenly complied. "The thing is, I think I could have feelings for him too. Or at least I think I might be able to, which is a big step up for me."

Mel looked for Maggie again. She checked the counter where she'd last seen the kitten. It was no longer there. Maggie had probably succeeded in coaxing it out.

Wherever the kitten was, there would be Maggie. The problem was the kitten was nowhere in sight. Mel ducked and turned and stood and craned her neck. The counter where she'd last seen them was near the open front door. The kitten could certainly have wandered out . . .

"I'm so pleased, dear," her mother was saying. "He is an adorable young man—"

"Oh my God!" Mel hung up abruptly. "I've lost his daughter!"

Along with his black morning coat and striped trousers, the doorman at Elizabeth Arden's on Fifth Avenue wore a yellow-and-black-striped silk vest. It made him look like the father of the bride, Jack thought, if the bride were a bumble bee. But the guy was nothing but polite. He hauled open the oversized red door and practically bowed as Jack followed a handsome gray-haired woman into the salon.

The softly lit white entrance hall with its marble, mirrors, and brass was steeped in fragrance, as if all the perfumed folds in a single fat issue of *Vanity Fair* had been opened at once. "I can help you?" a large Slavic woman standing behind a gleaming cosmetics counter asked Jack.

"I'm looking for Elaine Lieberman," he said, glancing down at the pink appointment book. "She's a customer—"

"Client," the woman corrected him, snapping shut

the book and clenching it firmly in her ample arms. "I am Rutta."

Jack bit back his inclination to say, "You certainly are," and took the smile out of moth balls.

"Rutta. Is that a Norwegian name?"

"Finnish," she said.

He was distracted. He was up there in his head, on-line and feverishly clicking through the menu, trying to find direct access to Lieberman's wife. "Finish?" he said, "What do you mean, 'finish'? I just got here," he complained, irritated now, hanging onto the smile by a thread. "And frankly, Rutta—" Then he got it.

"Oh, you meant the country. Finland. As in Finlandia? Nice country. Great vodka." He was losing ground. "Listen, Rutta. Excuse me, please. My name is Jack Taylor. You know, *You Don't Know Jack*."

She seemed stung.

"No, no, no, no," he explained. "That's my column. I write for a newspaper. *You Don't Know Jack* is what my column's called. Now, listen, I've got to see Mrs. Lieberman. It's an emergency—"

"Nobody goes into back rooms unless client or clinician," Rutta said.

Jack leaned toward her, readying himself for a more intimate, confidential approach. He turned up the smile.

Rutta smiled back at him. "Don't bother with the cute face," she said. "I got five sons. You make eyes at me like that, I make you pot roast; I don't interrupt Mrs. Lieberman during her facial."

Facial, facial, facial, Jack nodded. All he had to do now was find out which floor that would be. A handsome woman in a good Republican cloth coat stepped up to the counter.

"Excuse me," Rutta said to Jack, turning to her new client. "Hello, Mrs. Kempner."

"Certainly, of course," Jack said understandingly. Mrs. Kempner returned his smile, giving his ego a plaintive boost.

"Let me get your robe," Rutta was saying.

He backed away politely. Then, with seeming aimlessness, he meandered across the pale green carpeting toward the elevator and casually pressed the button.

The elegant car arrived moments after Rutta disappeared to fetch the amiable Mrs. Kempner's robe. Jack slipped aboard before the Slavic bouncer returned and, after hurriedly studying the floor menu inside the mirrored elevator, pressed eight.

The pastel world of facials, massages, and leg waxing was quietly humming along. There was no one at the eighth floor reception desk. He checked the appointment book and headed quickly for the room assigned to E. Lieberman.

Cautiously, he stuck his head in the door. A cadaverous old lady was having her upper lip waxed. "Elaine Lieberman?" Jack asked uncertainly.

The clinician glanced up. "You just missed her,"

she said. "I think she was on her way upstairs to Oribe's."

He thanked her, backed out of the room, hopped the elevator again, and headed up to the hair salon. As he stepped off the car, a lacquered matron, decked out in a stylish fiery pink suit, hid her haggard eyes behind a pair of enormous sunglasses and pressed the down button.

She needed the smile, Jack thought. Instinctively, he took the time to lavish it on her before asking the salon's redheaded receptionist where he might find Oribe. She indicated a door at the end of a well-appointed corridor. Jack thanked her and flashed an abbreviated version of the smile. She reacted nicely, he thought, and followed her direction to the small private room where the master was said to be styling.

"Hi. I'm looking for Elaine Lieberman," Jack announced from the doorway.

Oribe, blow dryer humming, appeared not to have heard him. His client, however, a pleasant older woman decked out in a salon robe, offered Jack a radiant smile and said, "Oh, you just missed her."

"Damn," said Jack.

"Jack? Is that you?" said the woman.

He cocked his head at her. "Yeah . . . ?"

"It's Rita. Mel's mother!" she greeted him, above the dryer's din.

"Rita!" He couldn't help grinning. She seemed utterly delighted to see him. She was just a bit plump, with enchanting dimples and familiar pale green eyes, and her face was charmingly flushed with the heat of Oribe's dryer.

"Can you believe what a small world it is?" Rita asked.

"I know," he told her. "I just took your grandson for a carriage ride in the park."

"So I heard," she said, clearly pleased. "That Sammy. He's cute, but what a handful. Anyway, I'm so glad you're here. I want to tell you something about my daughter, Jack. And it's something you may already suspect. Mel can make you want to scream like you're getting a full body wax."

Jack found himself nodding.

"She's that frustrating," Rita confided in her enthusiastic way. "But, inside, she's mush. You can scream, Jack, but don't run away too soon."

"Rita, I'd love to continue this," he confided, "but I'm in an incredible hurry. Was Elaine Lieberman wearing a pink suit by any chance?"

"Hot pink. Wasn't it gorgeous? Chanel, I think. It was Chanel, wasn't it, Oribe?"

"Damn!" Jack said again. "Listen, Rita, I've got to go!"

"You're adorable," said Rita, waggling her salon-spruced fingertips at him. "Go, sweetheart. Go ahead."

He took the steps two at a time. He bolted out a stairwell behind the startled Rutta. He crashed through the big red door onto the pavement of Fifth Avenue. He got there just in time to see Elizabeth

Arden's bee-vested doorkeeper settle Elaine Lieberman into the backseat of a waiting limo and wave her off into traffic.

Jack whipped out his cellular and started dialing. Nothing. He got nothing. No dialtone. No bim-bambing beeping of digits. Something was wrong with the phone. He banged it against his palm, and tried again. More nothing.

"Damn," he said. "Damn, shoot, and fudge!"

— Eleven —

Frantic did not begin to describe it. Mel had searched every cluttered inch of Serendipity and finally, grabbing Sammy's hand, had raced out of the restaurant and checked the street. "Maggie?! Maggie! Oh my God!" she hollered.

Right or left, left or right? Mel looked left toward the Roosevelt Island tram. There were just two stores in that direction, an antique shop and a wig store. Maggie was nowhere in sight. Mel turned right. "This way," she yelled at Sammy, as if she were leading a posse and not one bewildered child.

"Have you seen a little girl?" she asked the first person she encountered, and every single passerby thereafter. "Have you seen a little girl? Have you seen . . ."

Heads shook no. Tongues clucked pityingly. People's eyebrows went up, and then their hands, and they looked around, as if she'd asked for their wallets instead of whether they'd seen a lost child wandering alone on this impossibly crowded, probably dangerous street.

She scrambled onto the hood of a parked car and stood to get a better view of the street. "Maggie?! Maggie!!" She made a bullhorn of her hands and bellowed into the traffic noises.

Sammy stared up at her from the pavement, perplexed, embarrassed, awestruck. "Mommy, Mom? Did you lose Maggie?" he asked when she climbed down.

"Don't be silly," Mel admonished, kneeling, patting his head, kissing the chocolate smudge he'd missed when she'd sent him to wash his face and hands. "She's here. Somewhere. Come on, let's look in there."

Grabbing Sammy's hand, she ran to the entrance of the store to the right of Serendipity. "Have you seen a lost little six-year-old girl?" she called from the doorway.

The saleswoman, meticulously coiffed, wearing a flawless cocoa-and-rust ensemble, regarded her suspiciously. "You lost a child?"

Mel flinched, but nodded. "Haven't seen her, have you?"

The woman glared at her.

"Come on, Sammy." They hurried up the shallow steps to the street and continued west to the next store, a gourmet Italian food store.

"Have you seen a little girl?" Mel asked the elderly woman standing beneath a rack of dried and peppered salamis.

"You lost your little girl?" The woman crossed herself.

"She's just six years old," Mel explained, feeling tears begin to sting her nose. "She's very bright, very cute . . . very small."

The woman's pale forehead wrinkled in empathetic distress. She shook her head sadly.

Encouraged, desperate, Mel burbled, "She's not even mine, she's this guy I just met's kid. I told him all day how irresponsible he was, but he didn't lose my son. See, I've got my son," she said, raising Sammy's hand as proof. "But I lost his daughter!"

The next shop on the block was a boutique. "Have you seen a lost little girl?" Mel asked again, rushing across the plush carpet, and shouting over the bass-heavy reggae beat on the CD player.

The anemic white salesgirl in a long black tube dress with matching lipstick shook her head. Mel looked around tremulously, then suddenly grabbed a fringed pink suede thing off the rack and, dragging Sammy with her, ducked into the velvet-curtained dressing room.

Wide-eyed, Sammy watched in utter confusion as she hung the pink thing on the hook and got down onto her knees. The heavy dressing room curtains gave the little space the soothing privacy of a confessional.

"Dear God," Mel murmured. "I will never ask for anything else again as long as I live. Please, please, God, don't let anything bad happen to Maggie. Please just let me walk out of this store and there she'll be, and I will never be rude to anyone, or overly career driven again."

Out of the corner of her eye, she glimpsed her son's face. His puffy little mouth was agape. "And I won't just think of you when things get bad," she added abruptly. "I'll think of you all the time." She glanced again at Sammy. "And so will Sammy," she promised. "Amen. Say 'amen,' Sammy."

"What's amen?" he asked.

They'd gotten all the way to Third Avenue with no sight of Maggie. "Maybe we should run back and try the stores on the other side of Serendipity?" she said, wringing her hands.

The sight of a police car changed her mind.

"Stay here. Don't you move," she warned Sammy. Then, panic-stricken by the possibilities, imagining in an instant his disappearance, too, she grabbed his hand and ran with him out into traffic.

Waving her hands and weaving between cars, Mel reached the police cruiser seconds before the light changed.

An Officer Rodriguez drove them to the station house and an Officer Roberts took her statement. It was at his gray and scarred desk that she gave up hope of finding Maggie on her own, and tried to reach Jack.

"The cellular phone you have called is not answering at this time. Please try your call again later," was the message she got.

Roberts looked up from his computer. "Not there?" he asked, seeing her heightened distress.

She shook her head.

"Is there anything else you can tell us, Miss Parker?"

"I don't think so. I just . . . She was wearing a little purple jacket. Did I say that already?"

The policeman nodded patiently.

"And she's very cute . . . and little. I can't believe this happened."

"And you said you have no idea where the mother went for the honeymoon?" he pressed.

"No," she said. "Wait—somewhere warm. An island. Oh, God. It just happened so fast, you know? One minute she was there—"

Mel put her hands over her face and tried to breathe in shallow breaths. She was not ready to ask Officer Roberts if he had a paper bag she could use because she was hyperventilating. Undoubtedly the policeman, like everyone else in the busy, noisy, echoing precinct house, already thought she was a basket case. Which was very reasonable of them, really. Since she was.

Calm down, breathe, breathe, she told herself. Though you don't deserve to, said the critic.

"All right then," Roberts tried to console her. "There's nothing else you can do now."

Mel tore her hands from her face. "You don't understand, Officer," she managed to say before she began to sob. "I've ruined so many lives today!"

Her shoulders were shaking. Her nose was running. Sammy, who was a few desks away, thumping a processing stamp from a blue ink pad onto his hands, regarded her with a worried, embarrassed frown.

"I started off mean and pushy to my sister," Mel sobbed, "and I've been snippy to strangers all day, my boss is probably going to hate me and send me back to the drafting table because I'm never going to make cocktails by five-thirty, it's been raining all day and I'm a mess, and to top it all off I met a really cute guy who I was very haughty to, and then I lost his daughter!"

Officer Roberts pulled open his deep desk drawer and began rummaging through it. "Ma'am," he said gently, "we've got officers out there canvassing the neighborhood as we speak. Let us take care of it from here."

He pulled a paper bag from his drawer, shook out a couple of packs of gum and a bottle of aspirin, and handed the bag to Mel. "Here," he said gently, "breathe into this for a while. Nice and easy, shallow breaths."

4:15 P.M.

Celia was waiting for him at a pay phone in the lobby of the *Newsday* building. He shot out of the revolving door and headed straight for her. "My cell phone batteries are low," he said by way of greeting.

"Is that why you sent for me, Jack?" Celia fluttered her eyelashes at him. "Want me to jump-start your batteries?"

He showed her the digital message on his phone face. LOW BATTERY. "I need all the help I can get," he said, smiling. "I've been trying to reach Elaine Lieberman. Her maid answered twice. I tried to leave a message. I left my name. I'm going to call her again now. I need you to run interference for me in case Lieberman's maid picks up again, okay?"

"Anything for you Jaacck," Celia crooned.

He squeezed past her into the booth, dropped a quarter in the phone and dialed Lieberman's house.

"Hello?" said a very New York born and bred voice.

"Hello," Jack began.

"Jack Taylor?" the woman asked.

"Yes," he said, startled.

He heard her sigh. "Good. This is Elaine Lieberman," she announced.

Celia's eyebrows were raised questioningly. Jack nodded at her. Elaine Lieberman, he mouthed. Then he cleared his throat. "Mrs. Lieberman, this is Jack Taylor. *Newsday*," he said officially.

"I know," said Elaine Lieberman. "You're the one who wrote those articles about the Mayor taking kickbacks, right?"

"Well, Mrs. Lieberman—"

"Call me Elaine. Please," she insisted. Her words were curt, almost angry, yet there was a chilling note of pleasure in her voice as well. She seemed maliciously pleased to be speaking with him.

"Thank you," Jack said. He expected an argument, even a diatribe. When it didn't happen, he moved quickly into his own agenda. "I wanted to ask you a bit of a difficult question, er . . . Elaine," he ventured.

"About my husband?" There it was again, that angry delight.

"I'm not sure how much you know about his business affairs, but—"

"He's on the take," Elaine Lieberman announced warmly.

"Hang on, hang on. Please." Jack fumbled for his notepad. "Celia," he hissed, pointing to his cell phone, "can you get me a battery for this? Pretty please?"

She blew him a kiss and clacked away across the marble lobby floor.

"Okay, now, you were saying," said Jack.

"Elliot's on the take. The mayor's on the take. The City Comptroller's on the take . . ."

He was scrawling like mad. "I don't suppose you'd be willing to—"

"Go on the record with this?" she finished his thought.

"I know it's a lot to ask, but—"

"Elaine Lieberman," she said, then spelled out her name for him. "That's for the record," she said. "I have only one request."

"Anything," said Jack.

"Fax him a copy in Barbados."

"You've got it." He listened, scribbling everything into his notepad, flipping pages, shaking his cramped writing hand, switching phone ears. She gave him everything, the whole who-what-where-and-when. She gave him names, dates, places, amounts, checking-account numbers. She volunteered to mail him Elliot's bank statements and the notebook she'd slipped out of his briefcase the night he was packing for Barbados.

Hal wandered by the booth eating a large sandwich. He saw Jack and stopped, pleased.

"So basically, they're depositing the bribes or kickbacks or whatever you want to call it into Aikens' re-election campaign fund. That's how they wash the money," Elaine Lieberman concluded. "Is that right, wash the money?"

"Launder," Jack said.

"Yeah, that's what I meant. So is that enough?"

"Mrs. Lieberman, you have saved my life," he shouted.

"Lieberman?" Hal asked, when Jack had hung up, "as in, the Sanitation Commissioner's wife?"

"Hal, I got it. I got my source. I got my story back. Hal, I love you!" Jack said, grabbing the fat man's arms and dancing him around. "I love this city! I love this job! I love Elaine Lieberman!"

Hal held onto his sandwich protectively, and twisted his shoulders out of Jack's grip. "That's a lot of love for you, Jack," he laughed. "You haven't got something going with Mrs. Lieberman, have you?"

"Elaine? No. But I've got to tell you something, Tonto. I've got my eye on someone—"

"Not Celia," Hal said. "I was kind of hoping to show her my sensitive, brutality-loving side."

"Lots of luck, but no, it's not Celia. It's someone I just met . . . I mean, like, today."

"Not the witch?" Hal tore into his sandwich.

"The witch?"

"The one who said your marble was fudged."

"Yeah, that's her," Jack said grinning. "She's . . . I don't know how to describe her, Hal. She's . . . luminous," he decided. "Her face glows like I've never seen a face glow before."

"This morning you would have just said, 'She was hot. Done.'"

"Yeah, I know. It's weird, right?" He glanced at his watch.

Hal shrugged. "A lot can happen in a day."

"I've got to get down to Aikens' press conference. Hey, lend me your Motorola battery," Jack said. "I sent Celia upstairs, but I've got to get out of here."

Holding the sandwich in his mouth, Hal unhooked his cell phone and handed it to Jack, who pried out the battery. "Tell Celia thanks anyway. I'll try to check in with her from the cab. Later, Tonto."

"*Hasta la vista*, cowboy."

4:30 P.M.

"Mommy," Sammy said, "how long do we got to stay here, Mom?"

His hands were blue. The soap was blue. The enamel sink basin in the precinct house bathroom was blue. And Mel was blue—B.B. King, Billie Holiday, down there in loss and despair land blue.

"We have to wait until they find Maggie, honey," she said, fighting back tears again. She reached into her bag, pulled out a handkerchief and wiped Sammy's hands with it.

Most of the ink from the stamp pad he'd been playing with was off now. All that was left were little blue half-moons around his cuticles and under his fingernails. It was good enough, Mel decided. She blew her nose in the wet blue-stained handkerchief.

"What if they don't find her?"

"Don't even say that. Don't even think it," Mel urged. "Don't worry, Sammy, they'll find your little friend."

"I don't care if they don't," Sammy said sullenly. "She thinks she's so smart."

Mel took his hand and hurried back to Officer Roberts' desk. "Anything?" she asked.

"Not in the past two minutes," he said.

"You want me to sit down over there, don't you?" Mel asked meekly.

"That'd be nice," the policeman said. "There's nothing else to do, really. They're looking for her now. You can just relax."

"Just relax," Mel repeated, shaking her head morosely.

He handed her a tissue from the box on his desk and pointed to his nose. "Ink," he said kindly.

Mel wiped the ink off her nose. "Just relax, Sammy," she passed the suggestion on to her son who was testing the sharpness of the message spike on Roberts' desk.

"Don't worry," the cop said kindly.

"Don't worry, Sammy," Mel said.

"I'm not worried, Mommy."

"Well, I am," Mel rasped at Roberts. "Oh, please, isn't there something I can do instead of just sitting here? If only I could let him know. You know, let Maggie's father know what's happening—"

"You've been phoning him every five minutes—"

"Oh my God, it's four-thirty already. It's been, what?"

"Maybe twenty minutes?" Roberts answered. "Please, Miss Parker—"

"Four-thirty?" Melanie remembered. "He's got to be at the press conference at five! He'll be at City Hall in half an hour. Come on, Sammy, let's go."

"Miss Parker, it's probably better if you just wait

here. We'll probably have word soon—"

"I've got to let him know. I'm sorry. Thanks for everything. I'll be in touch," Mel shouted and, dragging Sammy behind her, sprinted for the door.

— Twelve —

"How do you like this day?" the cab driver said, as Jack settled into the back seat.

The sky was overcast again. People were moving even faster than usual through the midtown streets. Heads down, collars up, umbrellas at the ready. In fifteen minutes offices, factories, and showrooms would begin to spew their huddled masses onto the already bustling streets.

The furious walking race to Port Authority and Grand Central would begin. In a fever to escape the city, Reeboked secretaries and their Florsheimed mates would jostle, twist, and push past the incense dealers, camcorder tourists, Gap shoppers, and the-ater-goers in Times Square.

Traffic was already in misery mode. Taxis clogged the bus lanes, buses cut into the car traffic, limos bar-reled into the bike lane. And pedestrians wove wildly through the mess, mistaking Wait for Walk and Don't Walk for Run.

In the back of the cab, Jack snapped Hal's Motorola battery into his phone. The warning light went off. "It's beautiful," he told the driver, who'd already pulled out into traffic. "I love this day. City Hall, please."

Jack whipped out his notepad and flipped through it, grinning. "Yep, yep, yep," he murmured. "It is one fine day."

"You gonna sue somebody?" the taxi driver quipped.

"Excuse me?"

"It's an old saying. You know, 'Go sue City Hall.' You never heard that?" The cabbie shook his head. He picked up a folded newspaper and glanced at it as he drove. "You're probably not from New York, right? Probably don't even read the *Times*."

Jack leaned forward. "What're you reading? Is that Frankly Speaking?"

"Sure," said the driver. "You never read it?"

"You like that Frank Burroughs guy?" Jack asked.

"Yeah. He's very smart. I like his use of language. And you can really tell he's not stuck up or anything."

Jack nodded with resignation. "Because of the hat, right? Because of the Yankees cap, that's how you can tell?"

The cab driver was impressed. "Hey," he said.

"That's it. I couldn't put my finger on it, but that is it."

"Yeah, I'm smart, too," Jack said.

His mobile rang. He clicked it on. "Jack Taylor," he said.

"Mr. Taylor, we've found your daughter, sir," a stranger said.

Jack pulled the phone away from his ear and stared at it for a second, then pressed it back against his ear. "Who is this?" he demanded.

"This is Officer Roberts," the man said. "She's fine, Mr. Taylor. I just got a call from one of our officers on East Sixtieth Street. Your daughter is just fine. Apparently, she followed a kitten into a store. She's in a little antiques place between Second and Third on the north side of the street. It's one door east of Serendipity. You know that shop?"

Jack scrawled the address into his pad, then shouted it to the driver. "And fast!" he said. The cab swerved left, cutting off an entire lane of traffic, hung a squealing right and headed uptown.

Jack phoned Celia. "Can you cover for me at City Hall, stall as long as possible?" he asked, after explaining what had happened.

"She lost your daughter? What kind of woman is she?" Celia responded, shocked.

"No time for that, Celia. Hit it, get there, go!"

Jack jammed a fistful of bills into the driver's hand and jumped out of the cab in front of the antique store.

The interior of the shop was musty and chaotic. But in a dim, peaceful corner, amidst gilt mirrors, dusty canvases, verdigris angels, and oriental rugs, Maggie sat on the floor with three kittens in her lap. Next to her, in a rocking chair, a handsome old lady with snowy white hair sat watching her lovingly.

"Hey, Maggie Magpie, you crazy, runaway kitten chaser, you!" Jack called. "I'm Jack Taylor, Maggie's Dad," he introduced himself to the white-haired woman.

The store owner stood and took Jack's hand in hers. "Victoria Bach. You must have been wild with concern," she said softly. "I asked if her friend's mother knew she was here with me and the kittens. Maybe she didn't understand me. She nodded her head, so I thought it was alright. Until the police-woman came in, of course."

"Thank you so much for watching her," Jack said.

"It was my pleasure."

"Come on, Maggie, let's go," he said, bending down to swoop up his daughter. "We've got to hurry."

To Jack's surprise, instead of leaping up into his arms, Maggie pulled back. "No, Daddy," she said softly but definitely. "I want to stay here with the kittens."

"You can't play with the kittens now, Maggs. I've got a press conference."

She stared at him, then shook her head.

Jack's heart was racing. He was on Go. He was on

Go in a big, adrenaline-soaring way. It was nearly five o'clock and he was totally pumped with the Lieberman break. He could taste glory. It was a couple of miles downtown, just waiting for him. Frank Burroughs could wear a Yankees cap, a Knicks jacket, a Mets shirt and an Islanders cup—but he didn't have the story. Elaine Lieberman hadn't called Burroughs. She'd called big Jack. Cowboy Jack. The baddest muckraking mutha in the Big Apple!

"Tag!" Jack yelled at Maggie, touching her arm with manic energy. "Tag, you're it, Maggie noodle-doodle." He feinted toward the door. "Come on, chase me. You're it!" He had one foot facing the street, the other bent and ready to sprint, and his torso pretzeled around trying to get her to move. "You're it, Maggie. You know how to play. Come on!"

"I don't want to play with you," she said firmly. "I want to play with the kittens, Daddy."

"Red light, green light, one two three!" he teased. "You can't catch me! Please oh please oh please oh please oh please—" He started to tickle her.

She didn't laugh. "Stop it, Daddy," she demanded.

"Maggie," he said, falling to his knees in front of her. "I'm begging you, get off the floor and let's go now." A big gray puffball of a cat rubbed against his pants. Jack stood abruptly. "I mean it," he said. "Don't you understand? If I don't go now—" He threw his hands up. "Okay, okay, is that what you want? You want me to lose my job?"

Quick tears sprang to her eyes. She looked up at him and shook her head no. Her shoulders fell. Her plump little fingers very gently began to move the kittens off her lap and, defeated, she started to get up.

Jack took a deep breath, then crouched down to his daughter's level. He was still wired. His heart was still beating loud and fast, his muscles were tensed. But the sight of Maggie's dewy eyes, the slump of her fragile shoulders, took the fight out of him. "You love those kitties, huh?" he asked, feeling like a jerk.

Maggie nodded silently.

Jack sat down, cross-legged, opposite her. "You know their names?" he asked her.

Maggie nodded. For the first time since he'd come in—since he'd burst into the shop to rescue her and save his career in one fell swoop—his very small, probably frightened, kitten-loving little daughter smiled at him. "That one's Bob," she said, " 'cause he looks like a bobcat. Right?" She looked up at the old woman. "Right, Victoria?"

"Yes, dear," Victoria Bach said. "Would you like some coffee or tea?" she asked Jack. "I'm just going to run to the deli around the corner for a moment."

"Nothing, thanks," said Jack.

She read his thoughts, his look, he guessed. "Don't worry," she said. "If you want to leave, just pull the door shut. I've got my keys."

"And that's Fluffy," Maggie pointed to a chip off

the old gray puffball block. "And that one's, um . . . I forget that one's name."

Jack drew out his handkerchief and wiped Maggie's tear-stained face. One of the kittens she was holding nipped at his finger. Jack rubbed the little cat's bony and delicate mouth, and the kitten licked his finger.

"Look, Daddy." Maggie giggled. "He likes you!"

Jack put away the handkerchief. "Are you ready to go yet?" he asked gently.

The giggling stopped abruptly. Maggie's smile disappeared. She shook her head no.

Jack took a breath. He reached into his jacket pocket. The marble was there, cool, smooth, reassuring. He felt his breast pocket. His notepad was solid. He had the story. It wouldn't go away. He had the goods on the bad guys. He had the Mayor, the Comptroller, the Sanitation Commissioner, the head of Aikens' re-election committee, and a sprinkling of known and not-so-known mobsters.

There was no way he was going to make it to the press conference now. If Lew wanted to replace him with that long-winded, cap-wearing phony bastard, Frank Burroughs, fine. Cowboy Jack would just collect his Pulitzer across that big river in Jersey.

Jack relaxed. He looked at his child. What a heartbreaking little beauty she was, his Maggie, still delicate and small. And he remembered when she was even smaller, when he could, and had, held her in one hand. When bald and toothless, with a grin that spread across her entire face and his whole heart, she'd take his little finger into her mouth just like the raspy-tongued kitten had.

"Okay, Maggie," he said, feeling calmer now or, at least, willing to feel calmer, ready to let the wild energy that was his working oxygen seep away. "We'll stay here, then. We'll just stay here."

5:00 P.M.

There was a podium set up at the top of the steps leading to City Hall. A man in a baseball jacket was doing a sound check on the mikes. "Hello, hello . . . can you hear me, Al?" he said. "One two three, are we good? How's that?"

A crowd of reporters was gathered on the steps and sidewalk beneath him. News crews jostled for angles, chose their spots, checked their equipment. On-camera reporters blotted their makeup, examined their teeth for lettuce or lipstick, and gave their hair a final spray. Print people, newspaper and magazine stringers, city beat reporters and columnists checked their notes and notepads, circulated, gossiped, laughed, bitched, and speculated.

About half the men were in baseball jackets emblazoned with network and local news logos. The rest were wearing belted raincoats, some with hats. "Excuse me," Mel asked one of the raincoat crew. "Have you seen Jack Taylor anywhere?"

The man shook his head and resumed his conversation with an earnest young reporter with wings of stiff blond hair.

"I don't see him, Mom. Boy, he's going to be mad at you, huh?" Sammy was jumping up, trying to find Jack in the tall crowd.

A confidently attractive girl in very high heels and a very short skirt was dazzling two TV crew members. The men were laughing, talking, vying for her attention. The girl was looking past them, scanning the crowd. Her bored eyes fell momentarily on Mel.

"Excuse me, um, you wouldn't happen to know Jack Taylor would you?" Mel asked.

"Very well, in fact," the girl said, her eyes suddenly alive with questions of her own.

Her voice was familiar, deep, sultry, confident. "You're Celia, aren't you?" Mel said.

"Yee-es." Celia was looking her up and down, evaluating Mel with all the subtlety of a Rikers Island prison guard greeting a first-time offender.

A moment of horrified revelation cut short the appraisal. "And it's your fault Jack isn't here, isn't it?" said Celia. "How could you have lost his daughter? If he misses this press conference he can kiss his career goodbye."

A loudspeaker whistled with a piercing moan. "The Assistant Comptroller of the City of New York . . ." a man at the microphone said.

Celia turned away, shaking her head in disgust. Mel started to cry.

"What's the matter, Mommy?" Sammy asked. He'd been gathering muddy, nostril-sized acorns from a patch of wet grass.

Mel snuffled, blew her nose, tried to smile. "Those are excellent acorns," she said miserably. "Give them to me, sweetie. I'll hold them for you." Then she burst into tears again.

"It's okay, Mom. Honest. You can have them. They're for you."

A chubby, balding, nervous wreck of a man was gripping the podium with white knuckles. "Unthinkable," she heard him say. " . . . A family man . . . honor and respect . . ." And then he said, "Jack Taylor."

Mel blinked up at him, stood on her tiptoes, tried to keep the man in view over the heads of milling reporters and sound people waving booms, and flashbulbs popping and cameras held high. "Who's that?" she asked a denim jacket with a press pass dangling from its neck.

"Manny Feldstein, Taylor's alleged source," the man said.

"And in conclusion," Manny Feldstein was saying in a very shaky voice, "let me repeat that I have been falsely reported as a source in Mr. Taylor's column. I never spoke to Jack Taylor on this issue."

He was reading from a piece of paper hidden by the podium. At the mercy of the early evening breeze, its white edges kept fluttering into and out of sight.

"I've never even met Jack Taylor and I think it is highly unethical of him to have attributed remarks to me that I simply never made. Thank you," said Manny with visible relief.

A big man in a dark overcoat immediately led Feldstein away as reporters began to shout questions at him. A woman in a burgundy suit stepped up to the podium to distract them. "Aikens' press secretary," the denim jacket told Mel.

"Excuse me, excuse me!" the woman shouted. "People. Mr. Feldstein is not taking questions at this time. Mayor Aikens will be glad to entertain your questions in a moment. People!"

Mel craned her neck and saw Manny Feldstein quickly pop a pill into his mouth and stuff a fat prescription bottle back into his pocket before his companion helped him into a waiting car.

"It is now my pleasure to present Mayor Aikens," said the press secretary.

Mel looked around desperately. In increasing panic, she peered between shifting bodies, hats, and hairdos. Jack was still nowhere in sight. She strained toward the subway which was disgorging a new wave of harried riders but didn't see him among them. Things were moving along too quickly.

Mayor Aikens was entertaining the crowd. There was laughter and occasional applause. Now he was saying, "Thank you. Thank you very much. I appreciate all your support—especially in light of the ridiculous allegations made by Jack Taylor in his aptly named column, 'You Don't Know Jack.' "

There was a roar of laughter from the crowd. Mel cringed. It was the same line she'd used on Jack this morning. That was when she'd thought he was arrogant, insufferable. Before she'd seen his vulnerability. Before, actually, she'd ruined his entire life. Sammy tugged at her hand. "Mom. What did he say, Mom? What did he say about Jack, Mom?"

"Oh God, he's really not going to make it," Mel said, again trying to snuffle back tears. "Do you see him anywhere, Sammy? It's almost over."

"Questions?" Mayor Aikens called.

Mel jumped up, threw her arm in the air, waved wildly.

"Mom?!" Sammy gasped.

Aikens surveyed the familiar crowd. His eye settled quizzically on her. "Yes?" he shouted, pointing at Mel.

"Er . . . yes," she began.

Directly behind her, a voice boomed out, "Do you plan to sue Jack Taylor or *Newsday* . . ." The man in the Yankees cap stepped forward, squeezing her out of the way. ". . . for the apparently false and certainly unsubstantiated allegations they've made against you, Mr. Mayor?"

Mel turned to her denim-jacketed guide. "Frank Burroughs, *New York Times*," he told her.

"Say, that's not a bad idea," Mayor Aikens laughed.

*   *   *

It was all over in fifteen minutes—the speeches, jokes, jabs, and questions. Aikens left, grinning, shrugging in mock helplessness, waving over his shoulder as if the phalanx of bodyguards and functionaries were secreting him away against his will. The burgundy-suited press secretary handed out transcripts of his statement and Manny's. The reporters sprinted back to their vans and cabs. On the abandoned steps, city workers began to dismantle and remove the press conference trappings. Now all that was left was the cleanup crew.

And Mel. She sat with Sammy on the steep steps, dwarfed not only by the tall columns behind them, but by her own guilt, misery, and defeat. She would try the police station again in a moment. She would try Jack's cellular after that. And, if it was still not working, his office. Or she'd look up his home number. She just needed a moment, one small, quiet moment, free of tallying up the damage she had done.

She could not even think of Maggie without tears flooding her eyes and a pain so deep in her chest that she'd have gone to an emergency room if she had any remaining instinct for survival.

Sammy was poking at his shoe with a twig he'd found. It was broken but had sharp edges. Mel briefly reviewed the disaster potential of the stick. Considerable, she decided. Reflexively, she reached into her bag, drew out two action figures, took the stick from Sammy, and handed him the Power Ranger and Ninja Turtle.

"Almost time for my soccer game, Mom." He banged the toys together. "Look, Mom, Maggie," he said.

Mel glanced up listlessly.

Jack and Maggie were walking toward them. Maggie was holding the little kitten from Serendipity. "All the people are gone, Daddy," she said.

"That's alright, sweetheart. We'll get 'em tomorrow," Jack answered.

Mel jumped up. "Thank God you found her!"

"She was in the antique store next to Serendipity's," he said. There was no anger in his voice. In fact, he seemed more relaxed than he'd been all day. And more attractive.

"Thank God," she repeated. "I've been sick worrying about her. We looked everywhere. We went to the police station—"

"Look, I got a kitty," Maggie interrupted proudly. "His name is Bob and my Daddy said I could keep him."

Just hearing Maggie's voice again, letting it register that she was really here, really alright, released the pain around Mel's heart. She knelt down and touched Maggie's hair, then touched the kitten. "I'm so sorry about what happened to you, sweetheart. You must have been so scared. Are you okay now?"

Maggie nodded.

Mel looked up at Jack. "I'm so sorry, Jack. I can't tell you how awful I feel," she said, standing up again.

Sammy tugged at her skirt. "Mommy, are we going to the soccer game now?"

"Yes. Yes we are." To Jack she said, "We really should start heading over there. Are you and Maggie going?"

"We are," Jack said. They started to walk uptown together.

"Keep your eyes out for a cab," she said.

Several occupied taxis went by and a couple of buses. On one was a huge advertisement that read, "Frankly Speaking every day in the best newspaper in the world. *The New York Times.*"

With a surge of annoyance, Mel saw the face of the man who had silenced and shoved past her during the Mayor's press conference. "Frank Burroughs," she muttered.

Jack hadn't heard her. "That's the guy who's going to get my job thanks to—"

"Thanks to what?" she demanded defensively.

"To this insane day," he said. "It's just been one thing after another. My ex-wife, the Circle Line, Manny Feldstein, Frank Burroughs, Elaine Lieberman, Maggie getting lost . . . no one would believe this day."

"I would," Mel said, scanning the rush hour traffic for a cab. "Every day's like this for me. And I really don't think you need to insinuate that it was all my fault. Because for someone who's just lost his daughter, you seem pretty upset about your career."

"My career? As if your little presentation this

morning wasn't a priority. Hey, guess what? I don't need you to remind me about what comes first. I know what comes first, don't I Maggs?" He stroked Maggie's forehead, and she smiled up at him happily.

Mel glanced at Sammy. He shook his head, disappointed in her. If there was scorekeeping going on, he'd given the point to Jack. Who now added suddenly, "And by the way, I didn't 'just lose my daughter.' I just found her! I don't even want to think about what could have happened to her."

Mel was immediately abject. "I know. You're right," she said.

"But when I do think about it," he snorted arrogantly, "I can't believe that I was issued shellfish and animal dander warnings, sandbox alerts, commercial television guidelines. And you even laughed in my face when I arrived at your office on time, and then you lost my daughter."

"I know." Mel stopped, faced him, faced the music, looking directly into his warm brown eyes—which was not easy. Well, actually, it was too easy; much, much too easy and terribly disconcerting. "It was the worst thing I could have ever done," she confessed. "I'm really so, so very sorry."

The tiniest tilt of his lips hinted at a smile. "I'm not the irresponsible one, am I?"

Sammy was watching her, wide-eyed, hopeful. She could practically feel him wishing, rooting for her to say the right thing. "No," Mel admitted, to her son's relief and approval.

"I'd like to hear you say it. Say it for your kind."

"My kind?" Mel repeated, aghast.

Sammy bit his lip.

"Yeah, you know. The ones with all the balls up in the air," Jack said recklessly. "It's the least you could do."

Mel touched Sammy's curls lightly, trying to assuage his anxiety and, at the same time, distract him. No dice. "Of course I'll say it." For Sammy's sake, she thought. "I was the irresponsible one."

"Now say: I can't do everything alone." Jack's smile sneaked out of hiding.

"Why?" Mel demanded with the slightest grin.

"Because in one sentence you could restore my faith, perhaps even my interest, in women."

Maggie had joined the contest and was looking at her father questioningly.

"Well of course I'll say it for you, Jack," Mel equivocated, stepping off the curb suddenly, intently searching for a cab. "We're never going to get a cab, you know. Just as long as you realize that it won't be true," she added.

"You can't say it," he called after her.

"Of course I can." She glanced over her shoulder and threw him a phony smile.

"I'm waiting," he said.

"I can't do everything alone," she called, then added more quietly, "even though my daily activities year after year immediately contradict what I just said."

It started to drizzle again. They were in the middle of Chinatown now. The streets were narrower, crowded with shoppers.

"Thank you," Jack said.

Fruit and vegetable stalls jutted out into the street. Pink and gray fish, baskets of astonishing blue and red crabs and gray clams sat in melting ice. Wind-up toys skittered through the puddles and debris. Roasted ducks hung upside down in store windows.

Jack took Maggie's hand and then Sammy's, and they stepped out into the street.

"You made me grovel for no reason," Mel accused him. She could feel her hair frizzing up in the light rain.

"For great reason," he protested. "You are an arrogant ball juggler."

Mel spun around indignantly. "If you don't want your balls juggled, don't throw them in my face," she shouted.

Two elderly Chinese men squinted curiously at her through their cigarette smoke. She drew herself up abruptly. "Come here, Sammy," she said, holding out her hand for him.

He shook his head. "I want to walk with Jack."

"You can't. He's my Daddy," said Maggie.

"I never threw them in your face." Jack waved his arms wildly at an available taxi wedged in the five-lane traffic of Canal Street. A man in a Homburg hat and British umbrella dashed through traffic and nabbed the cab. Jack threw up his hands. "I give up!" he shouted.

"You did so," Mel called to him. They made their way through the traffic jam between stopped cars and streaming pedestrians. "Starting off this morning when you thrust your stupid column at me as some sort of lame excuse for making my son miss his field trip," she continued, the moment they were all safely accounted for on the Little Italy side of Canal.

Jack shook his head at her.

"Ho, ho, ho, big Jack reporter," Mel jeered, "can't possibly concentrate on mundane details like picking up a phone to say thanks anyway, but I won't be needing you to take my daughter to school today. Balls in my face, Jack!"

A woman in a black shawl and orthopedic shoes shook her head at Mel, and crossed herself.

"Then you have to ask, who I can only assume is one of your many girlfriends, if she's wearing her panties, just about as loud as you can so you're sure I won't miss a word. Balls in my face. And now, in the midst of my obvious and very deep remorse, you make me grovel?" She shook her head and blew back her hair. "Balls in my face," she concluded.

"Is that what you think? That's what you really think, huh?" he said.

She gave him a look—and there were those eyes again, squinched up but startlingly green just the same. And that pugnacious yet delicate chin, lifted.

"First of all," he said, disarmed, "I *thrust* my column in your face because I thought you were the most beautiful woman I'd ever seen and I wanted to make a good impression."

That rocked her. He pressed his advantage. "I forgot to call you this morning because I, as diametrically opposed to you, am not used to doing everything myself. So I slipped up there."

"Panties," she said.

"I was getting there. As for the panties, that remark was directed at my friend, Hal, simply to piss you off. Get that cab!" he hollered suddenly, then raced out into the street and did it.

"Damn, you almost ripped the door off," the driver said admiringly as they all piled into the back seat.

Mel let Sammy scoot in first, then followed him. Jack, mindful of the morning seating arrangements, slipped in beside her pulling Maggie and the kitten behind him. "Central Park South," he said.

Maggie leaned forward unexpectedly and whispered across the grownups to Sammy, "I think my dad likes your mom."

"Maybe my mom likes him back," Sammy confided.

"You know," Mel said to Jack, "men like you have made me the woman I am."

Sammy shook his head no at Maggie, and they sat back again.

"All the women I know like you make me think

that all women are like you," Jack retaliated.

"Oh my God, I almost forgot. I've got a meeting."
She turned to Jack. "It's drinks with clients."

"Mom." Sammy was upset.

"It's five-twenty-five," Jack said. "Rush hour.
You'll never make it."

"Mom, it's the last game of the season. It's for the
championships, Mom. And the coach said that every-
body has to play or you don't get a trophy. And even
the losers get a trophy. But you don't get a trophy if
you don't play, Mom."

She put her arm around him. "I know, Sammy, but
it's on the way. We'll make it."

"Let it go," Jack said gently. "It isn't worth it."

"I'm telling you I can do this." She leaned forward
and said to the driver, "Could we go to the 21 Club
instead?" She checked her Filofax. "Um . . . it's 21
West Fifty-second Street. Just don't try to take Fourteenth, Thirty-fourth, or Forty-second across because
you can't make a left at this hour."

Jack was shaking his head.

"You don't understand. I have to do this," she said
to him, then noticed that the cab was turning onto
Broadway. "Oh, don't take Broadway," she urged
the driver. "It's bound to be a mess. Try Sixth Avenue—but only after Twenty-third Street because of
the construction."

Now both the cabdriver and Jack were shaking
their heads at her. She didn't have the guts to watch
how Sammy was taking it. The cabbie heaved a sigh

of disgust, but followed her instructions.

"Great green globs of greasy grimy gopher guts," Jack sang softly to Maggie. "Mutilated monkey meat . . ."

Sammy stared sadly out the window which was slowly beading with raindrops.

"Don't take Forty-ninth," Mel ordered. "You'll hit all the traffic from the West Side Highway."

They pulled up in front of 21. Little iron jockeys in painted racing silks, each with one arm outstretched, lined an ornately railed balcony. The doorman reached out from under the awning to open the taxi door. Mel skittered over Sammy, stroking his face on the way, and hopped out. Then she peered back into the car. "Why don't you hold the cab and if I take longer than fifteen minutes, just go on ahead without me and I'll meet you there?"

Jack didn't appear to be listening. He was paying the driver. "You're going to take longer than fifteen minutes," he finally said, ushering the kids onto the sidewalk.

Sammy looked up at her nervously. "What if you don't come and daddy doesn't come?"

Mel took him aside and knelt down so that she was eye to eye with her small, worried son. "I'm going to be there," she promised. "Sammy, you're the most important thing to me in the whole world—"

"Your job is," he countered.

She was hurt. She tucked the feeling away into the nearly full repository of remorse in the pit of her stomach where the everyday little bruises and dis- appointments lodged. "Sammy," she said, tenderly, deliberately. "This has been a very bad day and I'm really sorry that I dragged you places and left you places."

His bottom lip, which had been sourly thrust for- ward, retracted slightly, forgivingly.

Mel smiled encouragingly. "I know I've been a yelling, screaming, running, crazy person, sweetie. But it's going to be better tomorrow and I promise I won't take longer than fifteen minutes in there, okay?"

Sammy nodded uncertainly, and Mel hugged him. "Thank you, thank you, sweetheart," she whispered, "I'll be right back." Then she shot Jack a pray-for-me look. He gave her a thumbs-up sign. And she hurried into the restaurant.

She swept past the noisy bar and searched the ex- pense account crowd at the tables. Smith Leland spotted her first. He waved sociably. The Yates men followed his lead, lifting their drinks to her as she picked her way through the busy restaurant.

"Glad you could join us," Kurt, the senior Yates, said. He made a half-hearted attempt to stand, then either second thought or poor coordination seated him again. "What are you drinking?"

Mel slipped into the banquette next to Leland. Out- side the large picture window at the front of the res- taurant, she saw Jack and the kids in conference.

"Oh, just water," she answered, with what she hoped would seem like a good-sport grin.

"Nonsense," Kurt insisted, "We're way ahead of you already. You've got to catch up fast." His heavy face was flushed and smiling, but Mel knew an order when she heard one.

Leland took over. "She'll have a dry vodka martini. Straight up," he told the waiter.

Mel glanced at the picture window again. She could see Jack checking his watch. And Maggie, beside him, contentedly playing with her kitten. And Sammy whose adorable little face was now totally focused on a pair of passersby—a father and son who were walking hand in hand. Sammy's expression was pensive, wistful. It just about broke her heart.

"Penny for your thoughts," Joseph Yates chuckled, calling her attention back to the business at hand. "Though we all know they're worth a lot more than that."

"They sure are." Smith Leland's arm fell heavily on Mel's shoulder and he laughed as though Joe Yates was the funniest, most original thinker he'd ever heard. "But don't you worry, our clever little gal here gets excellent compensation for those brilliant thoughts of hers. Melanie, Joe and Kurt were just thinking of throwing another project our way."

"Yes," Yates said, "We were just discussing plans for a sort of upscale amusement complex for adults."

Kurt added, "You know, with food and games and rides—"

"No rides, Dad," Joe corrected. "We want to keep the liability down and appeal to a high-ticket consumer base."

Melanie glanced at the clock over the bar, then turned a smiling face to the jovial Yates boys. It took everything she had not to look out the window again.

— Thirteen —

"We've still got about fifteen minutes to make it over to the park," Jack assured the kids.

"Okay, Daddy," Maggie said, without even glancing at him. Sammy didn't respond at all.

"So what do you say, how're we going to while away the time?" Jack tried again.

The boy tore his eyes from the back of a man walking along Fifty-second Street with his small son. He blinked up at Jack as if waking from a dream.

"What's up?" Jack asked gently. "What were you thinking?"

Sammy shrugged. "I really hope my daddy comes to our soccer game," he said, then added with uncertain pride, "Mommy hopes he's coming too."

Jack glanced in at Mel. She was in a banquette near the window, one of the power booths. Her gorgeous profile was tilted in the direction of a beefy gray-haired suit, an older man with a bad haircut and big grin. "You bet," Jack said, distracted.

"Last night she thought I was asleep, but I heard her say, 'Please let Eddie come, please let Eddie come.' That's what she kept saying."

Jack turned back to the boy. "Eddie? Who's that?"

Sammy looked up at him, perplexed, as if to say *Don't you know? Doesn't everyone know?* "Eddie's my dad," he explained.

"Oh, so your mom wants him to come to the game?" He hadn't expected the quick surge of disappointment that ambushed him. "Well, sure. Of course," he said.

"What time is it, Jack?" Sammy asked, worried again.

"We'll make it, buddy. Hey, let's see if we can tempt her out of there," he suggested. "Let's make faces at your mom; be so cute she can't resist, okay?"

"Yes!" Sammy's pessimism vanished. Even Maggie looked up from her kitten, pleased by the challenge, ready to play. "Can Bob make faces, too?" she asked.

"Definitely. Anyone who's irresistibly adorable can join in," Jack decreed.

As they moved toward the window, Leland looked up. He focused for a second on Sammy, then, puzzled, imperceptibly shook his head.

"After drinks, we wanted to take a drive out to Stamford," Kurt was saying, "And I thought maybe we could stop at Ben and Jerry's, too."

"Isn't that the little lost boy from this morning?" Leland pointed Sammy out to Mel.

"We were hoping to take a look at a bad version of what we had in mind," Joe Yates added.

"Are you with us, Smith?" Kurt admonished.

"Of course," Leland said, snapping back. "Er, Melanie—" He turned to her for help, but she was looking at the clock again. "What I was thinking," Leland vamped, "was . . . er, before we head out, Melanie, why don't you toss out a few ideas. Just off the top of your head."

She floundered for a moment, unable to speak.

"You know, just in general," Leland prompted.

"Well, let's see," Mel began. "Adult amusement complexes until now have been, er, somewhat . . ." She glanced at an enormous open-faced cheeseburger that had just been placed on the next table. "Cheesy," she said with authority. "They've usually been attached to popular video stores and such; however, what I'm thinking of is a bit more exciting."

The Yateses were leaning forward, spellbound, but Leland sensed her hesitation. "A drawing would help, don't you think?" he suggested.

"I love drawings!" Kurt said.

"Yes, of course." Melanie dug into her bag for a pen, then glanced at the clock again. She'd have to sprint for the door in about five minutes. She reached for a napkin and began improvising a drawing on it. "Okay, give me a minute. Alright, here's what I see—"

Looking up, hoping to clarify the image she'd conjured, she saw instead Sammy's face at the window. His lips were suctioned onto the glass and he was blowing into it so that his cheeks were ridiculously round and full. Beside him, Maggie was waving the little black-and-white kitten's paw at her.

A smile crept across Mel's face. Then she ducked her head and concentrated on the drawing again. A moment later, she checked the clock, glanced at the window, and this time saw both kids and Jack staring at her. Their eyes were wide and comically pleading, their faces grotesquely squashed against the glass.

She stopped drawing and put her pen down firmly on the table. "You know, I can't do this now," she announced. "And I can't go to Stamford with you now, either. And, yes, Mr. Leland, that is the little lost boy from this morning. Only he's not lost. He's my son. I've got a child and he's got a soccer game in ten minutes. If he's late, he doesn't get a trophy. And because I'm in here with you, he'll probably be late."

She stopped just long enough to smile and nod at the window faces. Then, before Leland could speak, she hurried. "But what gets to me more than anything is that instead of crying about it, he's out there with a big old smile blowing fish faces at us." She tossed the pen back into her bag and pushed away the napkin.

Kurt quickly picked up the drawing, glanced at it, and passed it to Joseph as Mel continued. "If you're smart, gentlemen," she said, "you'll want me as

much for my dedication and ability as for the fact
that I'm going to ditch you now and somehow get
uptown so that my kid knows that what matters most
to me is him."

Her hands had begun to tremble. Or maybe they'd
been shaking all along and she'd only just noticed,
and also noticed that she could hardly breathe.

She stood abruptly.

"Your real grounds for firing me, Mr. Leland,
should be if I were to stay here with you." She
hooked her black bag onto her shoulder, nodded to
Kurt and Joseph, and, on legs of Jell-o, turned to
leave—almost bumping into the waiter who was
bringing her martini to the table.

"Gentlemen," Leland began, furious.

"Now that's a spunky gal," Joseph said admiringly.

"Brains, beauty, and motherhood—that's what
America's all about," his father added.

Jack, Sammy, and Maggie were slapping high fives
when Melanie emerged from the restaurant. "It
worked, it worked," Sammy hollered.

"It was my daddy's idea," Maggie reminded him.

Mel made a fish face at them. Her audacity
stunned her, but the shakiness she'd experienced at
the table seemed to have vanished. Now, stepping
out into the daylight, however overcast and threatening, she felt suddenly and incredibly exhilarated.
"Well, I've probably just lost my job but at least we've

got—" She checked her watch again. "Oh my God, eight minutes to get to the game."

"I say we start running," Jack suggested buoyantly.

"Alright!" Sammy hollered.

"Want to run?" Maggie asked her kitten. "I'll hold you tight, okay?"

They jogged west toward Sixth Avenue. "In spite of everthing, Jack," Mel said on the run, "I want you to know that I do sincerely apologize for losing Maggie."

"And I accept." Jack took her elbow, moving her along. "Especially in light of the fact that the very same thing happened to me this morning."

The children skittered ahead detouring around startled pedestrians and pausing to inspect a table full of Russian dolls and artifacts set up in the shelter of an old brownstone building. A lanky young man holding an umbrella over the merchandise started to show them how the dolls came apart, each one brightly painted and hiding a smaller doll inside it.

"You lost Maggie this morning?" Melanie asked, keeping an eye on the kids.

"Yeah. She went off chasing after our office cat. Where is she?"

Mel pointed to the umbrella. "Really? So she does this all the time?" she teased. "It might have been helpful if you had mentioned it."

Jack smiled, then swooped up the children and got them headed in the right direction again. "You know," he said, as they rounded the corner, "it might have been helpful if you had mentioned Sammy's penchant for sticking things up his nose."

Sammy heard and glanced guiltily back at his mother. "Oh no," Mel said, almost laughing. "You didn't."

Sammy nodded, then hurried ahead as Jack fished the marble out of his pocket and showed it to Mel. "Way up there," he said, inhaling deeply. The frantic pace was taking its toll again. But she was keeping up with him, enormous black bag and all. And she was smiling, laughing, beautiful. From the tips of those shiny little high heels clicking alongside him to the top of her now wild, wind-whipped hair. "Had to go to the emergency room," he said, brandishing the magic marble. "The doctor yanked it out with pliers."

"It's called an alligator," she said, chuckling. They were sprinting toward the park now, only three blocks away. "It's a tool I've come to know well, believe me."

Suddenly, Maggie tugged at his raincoat. "I have to go to the bathroom, Daddy."

Jack slowed to scan the avenue. Between the streaming rush hour suits and noisily snarled traffic, he caught sight of a coffee shop across the street. "Over there," he shouted, like an urban wilderness guide. "Come on, I'll take you."

"Why don't I take her?" Mel suggested in a raspy little voice. She'd stopped running and, head down, inhaling in gasps, had one hand pressed against her rib cage. Superwoman, winded at last. Jack grinned happily at her and took her arm as Sammy grasped her other hand, and the four of them ran across the street.

"Sammy, you have to go, too?" Mel asked outside the coffee shop. He shook his head no. "You sure? Jack can take you while I take Maggie."

"No, Mom," Sammy said. "But hurry, okay?"

While she waited outside the stall for Maggie, Mel splashed her face with water and tried to tame her hair. She groaned glimpsing herself in the mirror. She couldn't believe she'd been in 21 with hair that would be considered big even by Nashville standards. In contrast to the trendy New York look of . . . "So, Maggie, you know that lady, Celia, from your Dad's office?" she found herself saying.

"Yeah," said Maggie.

Mel bit her lip, but hurried on. "Um, is she your Daddy's girlfriend?"

"No way," said the adamant little voice inside the stall. "She wants to be, but she isn't." This was punctuated by a flush and followed by Maggie's emergence. "He wants someone who would love his cookie, too," Maggie explained, as Mel helped her wash up, "and that Celia's not the type."

As they hurried through the coffee shop, they could see Jack and Sammy huddled in the doorway.

"And mom says that when she and daddy first met," Sammy was telling Jack, "he was the coolest guy she knew and that now I'm the coolest guy she knows. I'm going to be a musician, too, because they get all the best girls like mommy."

"Who gets the best girls?" Mel asked, grinning.

"Musicians," Jack told her, holding open the door.

"Oh." She barely heard his response, but gave him a big smile anyway. One for Celia, she told herself, so elated that she scarcely noticed the sad little grin Jack offered in return.

"So, no other catastrophes happened?" she asked as they raced into the park.

"Lois Lane ate the class fish," Maggie announced.

"Why does this not surprise me?" Jack muttered, beginning to suspect that his luck was turning. The secret Maggie was supposed to keep was out. Mel liked musicians. Clearly, his marble was losing its mojo.

"Sorry," Maggie said to Sammy.

"Lois Lane?" Mel asked.

— Fourteen —

"There it is, there it is," Sammy yelled, pointing in the direction of the flooded field where six-year-olds were milling in the mud and dozens of parents sat in the bleachers on newspapers and plastic bags.

A water-filled trench circled the soccer field like a moat. There was no easy way around it. The children, however, didn't hesitate. As Mel paused at the puddle's edge trying to find a solution, they ran through the water, splashing and kicking up as much mud as they could. "Sammy, stop," she said, then gasped as Jack took off his wrinkled raincoat and tossed it over the gulf.

"Oh, no. No." Mel laughed, but couldn't bring herself to step onto the coat. And suddenly, Jack swept her up in his arms and carried her across the trench as Sammy and Maggie giggled and shook their heads.

The children ran onto the soccer field. Jack set Mel down. His hands lingered at her waist. She was still laughing. She was flushed and girlish and very close. So close that he could see his own reflection in her remarkable pale eyes and feel her breath on his lips. "Daddy, Dad." Maggie was back. "Hold him for me," she said, handing Jack the kitten.

Melanie hadn't moved. "Maybe you and Maggie could come over for dinner after the game," she said. "We can order Chinese or something."

Sammy cried out suddenly, and they both turned toward him.

"Daddy! Dad! You came. You came, Daddy!" He was running across the field to Eddie.

"Thank God he's here," Mel said.

Jack's smile froze on his face. "Yeah, great," he said.

"So what do you say?" Mel turned back to him.

"Say?" He could hardly look at her, see those eyes again, almost taste her lips. What the hell had happened, he wondered, standing there with a phony smile plastered across his face. How had he fallen so fast and hard for someone who was still carrying a torch for her ex? "Oh, you mean dinner," he said at last. "I don't think so. It's been a long day."

"Oh." She seemed surprised, maybe even a little disappointed. But it didn't take her long to regroup, Jack thought. "Well," she said. "Sure. Okay. Yeah,

I'm pretty tired. Well. I guess I should go say hi to Sammy's . . ." She gestured vaguely in the direction of the handsome, long-haired, cool guy Sammy was dancing around and talking at in a feverishly up-beat rush.

"His dad," said Jack. "Yeah, well, I'm going over there." He pointed across the field, away from the bleachers, away from Sammy and his father. "I like to watch from the sidelines. So—" With a shrug, he let it trail off.

"Okay." Mel nodded, hanging onto a fragile smile. "Right, well."

"Yeah," said Jack, "Go. I mean . . . You know, er . . . Well, see you."

She gave him a look, a searching, very Sammy-like look, curious, innocent, vulnerable, then quickly turned and slogged across the patchy grass to the bleachers. Jack couldn't tear his eyes away. He watched her walk, saw her tug down her jacket, smooth her skirt, blow back her hair. Every gesture seemed strangely familiar to him; intimate, almost. He knew it was time to go or, at least, to walk away, head over to Maggie, turn his back, do something, anything, but stand there staring after her.

And then the guy, Eddie, the musician, the drummer, for Godsake, reached out and took Mel's chin tenderly in his hands.

Jack turned away abruptly. His gaze fell on the muddy raincoat stretched out like a martyred alter ego on the sodden ground. He stared at it distractedly for a moment, then turned to look for Maggie. She was running in circles with two other children. "Maggie Magpie," he called, trotting toward her. "Where's my girl?"

Mel heard him. With Eddie's hands still on her chin, she glanced in Jack's direction.

"What," Eddie said, "you can't even look at me?"

"Stop," she admonished. Sammy was nearby. Sitting on the bleachers changing into his cleats, he looked up at the two of them, his face aglow with pride. "This is the second game you've made it to in two years, Eddie," Mel said, pulling her face away.

"Look, I'm here, aren't I?"

"Dad?" Sammy called just then. "Are you staying for the whole game? Are you, Dad?"

"Sure thing," Eddie said. "You bet I am."

"Wow," said Sammy. "I'm going to play my best. You watch me, Daddy. My *really* best!" He leapt from the bench and ran happily onto the playing field to join Maggie and some of the other children who were charging through the mud after a bouncing soccer ball.

Mel regarded her ex-husband suspiciously.

"What?" Eddie said, eyes wide suddenly, wounded. "I said I'm staying, okay? I'm going to try to stay. Come on, I saved you a seat." He pointed up into the bleachers, showing her where his tour jacket was draped over a space for two.

Mel turned to look for Jack. He was across the field, near the coach's bench, pacing, totally engrossed in watching the kids tear after the ball. He was holding the kitten against that poor bedraggled jacket of his, the one that had sucked up the day's drizzle like a sponge. His raincoat, Mel noticed, was still lying where he'd tossed it.

It had been a sweet stunt, that raincoat thing, the way he'd swept her up in his arms, the unexpected warmth of his body, the closeness of his lips. Mel shook her head now and sighed. And like a prisoner mounting the steps of the gallows, she followed Eddie up into the bleachers.

She'd barely sat down when a balding, heavy-set young man she recognized as "Kyle's father, the litigator," put a whistle to his cherubic red lips and blew. The shrill noise halted the muddy scuffling and screaming for a moment. The litigator tossed out a clean ball. And the game began.

On the uneven, rain-rutted field, little children ran, slid, and shrieked, trailing after the black-and-white ball on legs that seemed at times as rickety as those of a young doe. Parents called out encouragement, cautions, advice. Sammy charged across the turf at top speed. Then, as the ball came toward him, he checked to see whether Eddie was watching. His father smiled and waved. And Sammy turned his back on the ball and returned Eddie's wave with all his might.

"Part of the reason I came today," Eddie told Mel, his smile still in place, "is to tell Sammy in person that I'm not going to be able to make our fishing trip this summer."

Mel's heart sank. "No," she implored. But the quick sting of tears irritated her nose and filled her throat. Instinctively, she turned her head away from the game and hid her face against Eddie's sleeve. She leaned close into him, so that no one would see her, no one but he would hear. "You can't do this to him, Eddie," she whispered urgently. "Can't you see how much he needs you?"

Eddie stroked her back awkwardly. "I've got a gig, Mel, touring with Bruce. I mean, it's major. Come on, you can't expect me to pass that up."

Across the field, Jack saw Mel and Eddie sharing a tender moment. Kitten in hand, he turned away abruptly and faced the wildly exuberant children. "Watch the alley, Maggs!" he hollered. He didn't know what he felt, disappointment, anger—whatever it was, it was now aimed squarely at shaping up this so-called soccer game, this disintegrating mud bath before him. "On your left. Your *left*!" he commanded. "Come on, Maggie. Now go! Go! Go!"

Obediently, Maggie lunged toward the ball and managed to kick it forward twice in a row. "Way to go, Maggie!" Jack yelled. There was a distant rumble of thunder as he punched his fist triumphantly into the air.

"Who is that man?" an L.L. Bean–outfitted young mother near Mel asked.

"Some macho jerk," another parent muttered.

"They're babies, for goodness' sake," one handsome matron offered.

Mel peeked out at the game. Above the field, darkening clouds scudded by. Below them, Jack was running up and down the sidelines, brandishing the kitten, and shouting out instructions to Maggie's team.

"Seriously," Eddie said, tilting Mel's face up to his. "Give me a break here, Mel."

She pulled free of him, but moved back again to whisper, "I cannot even imagine a bigger disappointment than you, Eddie."

"Yeah, well. Hey, look at the kid," he marveled.

Mel wiped her face on her jacket sleeve and turned in time to catch Sammy's moment of triumph. The soccer ball jogged toward him and he caught it with the inside of his right shoe and sent it spinning toward the goal.

Mel smiled through her tears at him and waved.

Jack glanced at her briefly, saw the tender, teary smile, and redoubled his sideline coaching efforts. "Atta girl, Maggie!" he yelled loud enough for Mel and every other parent in the bleachers to hear him. And to realize how totally involved he was with the kids. And how he couldn't care less about who was crying joyful tears of reconciliation. "You're doing great!"

The ball had landed directly in front of Maggie. A chunky little boy charged up to her and tried to kick it away. Jack sprinted along the edge of the field to-

ward them. "Don't let him take the ball! Body check
him, Maggs. Body check him!" Head down, shoulders in ramming position, Jack pantomimed what he
meant. Maggie looked over at him and rolled her
eyes.

"Shove him, Mag!" shouted Jack.

"But that's rude, Daddy," the little girl said.

"It's not rude!" he bellowed, "It's sports!" A Me-
phistophelean clap of lightning lit the scene.

Maggie shrugged and butted the hefty boy out of
the way. The boy slipped, fell backwards into the
mud, and began to cry. The stands were in a grum-
bling uproar, and a few other self-appointed sideline
coaches glared at Jack disapprovingly.

Then it began to rain.

Maggie hurried into Jack's arms, and took her kitten from him protectively. With a terrible sucking
sound, the fat boy was hoisted out of the mud by his
mother. Some children ran toward the bleachers
meeting their rain-gear-toting nannies and parents
halfway. Others splashed delightedly in the rain until
irate adults came to fetch them. In quick order, a trophy dispatching tent was improvised under the
bleachers and a line of eager young players formed
to collect their prizes.

Sammy was among them. Beaming, he accepted
the little plastic trophy. Then, waving it victoriously
above his head, he ran to his parents. Sheltering the
kitten inside his jacket, Jack waited for Maggie who
was next in line. Carelessly clutching her trophy, she

walked back to him and took his hand. "You were great," he said.

"You were bossy," she responded. "And everyone's going to be mad at me."

"Never!" Jack promised. "No one could be mad at you, my rainy, brainy, icky, sticky soccer sweetie."

"I know." She relented with a smile.

He picked her up and started slogging toward the Central Park West exit, near Tavern on the Green. At the edge of the soccer field, he stopped, turned, and saw Mel in the distance. Dampened but undaunted, he thought. She was pulling one piece of rain gear after another out of her magical mommy bag. Jack started to smile, then noticed her rock-and-roll ex hovering near. The guy's hair was soaked, and he was pulling it back into one of those executive ponytails. Jack shook his head, turned west again, and surprised himself by sighing.

"What's the matter, Daddy?" Maggie asked.

He pasted on a halfhearted grin, then jacked up the wattage. "I'm just so torn," he said. "I don't know whether we should get Alpo on our pizza or Nine Lives."

"That's a catfood, Daddy!" She giggled.

"No, that's a dilemma," he insisted.

Eddie gave Sammy a quick kiss goodbye. "Okay, champ. I've got to get back to the studio."

"Did you see me, Dad?" Sammy asked again, as Mel helped him into the trekker rain gear she'd

picked up on sale at Paragon two weeks ago. She'd
bought it in preparation for Sammy's summer fishing
excursion with Eddie. Now Eddie was out of the picture. And so was Jack, Mel noted, as she snapped
Sammy into the waterproof pants and jacket. He'd
left the soccer field, and she hadn't even gotten to
say goodbye.

"Sure I did. You were great." The incredible disappearing father tousled Sammy's hair. "See you,
kid," Eddie said, then turned toward her, primed for
a farewell kiss.

"Yeah, see you," Mel said, echoing his cavalier dis-
missal of Sammy. Eddie shrugged, smiled, shoved
his hands into his pockets, and sauntered off through
the rain—like Gene Kelly's evil twin, Mel thought.
He hadn't mentioned canceling the fishing trip, of
course. He'd saved that privilege for her.

Belatedly and with a vengeance, Mel snapped open
her umbrella. Then she took Sammy's hand and,
plodding through mud, headed east across the Sheep
Meadow toward home. She could cry all she wanted
now, she thought blinking against the rain. Her face
was so wet that no one, not even Sammy, would notice.

"What's the matter, Mommy?" he asked suddenly.

"I'm just tired, sweetie. Aren't you?"

He thought about it for a moment. "No," he said.
"Where's Jack?"

"He and Maggie are probably going home to his
house," Mel said, "and we're going home to ours."

"We could go visit them maybe," said Sammy. "I want to show Jack my trophy."

"He saw it, honey. He saw how well you played."

They were approaching the boating pond, which was empty, of course. "Did he say I was great?" Sammy asked eagerly.

"No, he was in a hurry . . . because of the rain. But I know he was proud of you, too. Hey, listen," she improvised, "you want to go for a row?"

"But, Mom," Sammy said, practical suddenly, "it's raining."

"What do you care? You're dressed for Niagara Falls."

They rented a boat from a man who never stopped shaking his head at them or spewing cliches. "No law against it," he said, "It's a free country. Do what you want. You want to row in the rain, you got it. Don't ask me. I just work here."

"What an old fart," Sammy said, startling her. They'd pushed off from shore and were heading out into the rain-pocked pond.

"Excuse me," said Mel, "that isn't very polite."

"So?" Defiantly, Sammy lifted his chin at her.

She was too weary for confrontation now. And much too wet. Her hair hung in strings around her ears. She could wring out her shoes. Sammy grinned at her suddenly. "I was just kidding, Mom," he said. Then he moved cautiously to the side of the boat and trailed his fingers in the water.

"Sammy," Mel began. "I don't know how to . . .

Sammy, listen, I figure it's better to tell you this right away so you don't spend too much time getting excited—"

He was alert at once, looking at her with those doe eyes of his.

"Your dad isn't going to be able to take you fishing this summer," she said.

"Why not?" He turned away and watched the water, generously releasing her from that achingly vulnerable gaze.

Mel swallowed hard, then cleared her throat. "He has to . . . he has to work really hard so that he can make enough money to take you fishing next year." The false gaiety she'd pumped into the lie appalled her, but Sammy nodded his head gravely, apparently accepting the lame excuse.

"But, hey," she said, ratcheting the fun up a notch, trying desperately to cheer him, "how would you like to go white water rafting with me?" She rocked the boat coyly. "How about that?"

Sammy regarded her skeptically.

"You go really fast and get really wet," Mel continued, "and it's really bumpy and sometimes you almost fall out! Does that sound like fun?"

A small thoughtful smile appeared on his face and gave way to a full-out grin. "Yeah!" he decided.

"Well, okay!" Mel said. Then, arms outstretched, she moved across the boat for Sammy, who happily tolerated her sappy, wet hug. Mel squeezed him. Her rain-cooled cheek burrowed past the stiff vinyl collar of his slicker until it unearthed his grimy, warm neck.

"Hey, Mom. Mommy. Hey, come on." Sammy squirmed and giggled in her embrace as the solitary old boat creaked and jiggled on the pond.

8:30 P.M.

With an ominous whistling sound, a red light rocketed into the night sky, lasered through the clouds, and exploded into a booming scarlet dandelion. Jack watched the burst of light bloom and die, faded petals trickling down toward earth.

"Did you see that, Dad?" Maggie asked, turning from the window to look up at him. A forgotten crust of pizza was clenched in her fist. Tomato sauce and cheese rimmed her mouth. "Boy, that was a big one."

"Excellent." Jack urged enthusiasm into his voice. "Isn't this great, Maggie Magpie? Fireworks just for us." He held out his hand for the pizza rind, and turned briefly back to the window. Another fireworks flower was blooming, green this time. He wondered if it was visible across town.

"Is there any more?" Maggie asked.

"Fireworks or pizza?"

"Pizza, silly." Maggie glanced down at the kitten curled and purring at her feet. "I think Bob wants some more."

"One slice of sardine pie, coming right up." Jack ducked under the scaffolding and crossed the living room to the coffee table. On it, an open pizza box sat aslant a pile of magazines, books, and ceramic mugs in which oily coffee slicks were aging. He tore a slice from the pie, took a bite of it, then tossed it into the empty flower pot in which his once mighty cactus had recently expired.

He was in a funny mood, he decided. Not funny ha-ha. Funny as in strange, odd, melancholy, morose. It had something to do with the rain, he figured. The relentlessly overcast day that occasionally had given way to torrential squalls had seriously dampened his spirit.

That was it, Jack decided, carefully separating an-other slice of pizza for Maggie. It was the weather. And her. Supermom. The former and possibly future Mrs. Cool. She'd gotten under his skin the way the rain had gotten into his jacket. She was on his mind and in his nostrils now. Like mildew.

"Think your friend Sammy can see the fireworks from his house?" he asked, bringing Maggie the piece of pizza.

She shrugged, took the slice with two hands, then yawned suddenly. "What are they for, Daddy?" she asked sleepily.

"The fireworks?" He glanced out the window. With a distant pop, two more flares opened, show-ering a strange green light over the rooftops of nearby buildings. "I don't know, Mags. Something special that we don't know about, I guess."

Maggie nibbled at the pointy end of her pizza, then

set the slice down on the window sill. "I'm tired, Daddy," she said, yawning again. "I think I'll go to sleep now."

Jack carried her over to the couch. "I'll tuck you in, sweetheart," he said, setting her down on the bed he'd made for her. She flopped over like a little bean bag and he shook out his quilt and covered her.

"I want my kitty, Dad."

Under the pipes near the window the little cat was licking a salty bit of anchovy that had fallen from Maggie's pizza. "Okey-dokey, smoky," Jack said, weaving through the scaffolding to get the kitten.

"You know, Daddy . . ." Maggie's furry voice followed him. "When me and Melanie were in the bathroom, she asked me if Celia was your girlfriend."

Jack grabbed the kitten and straightened up with such alacrity that the back of his head bonged against a pipe. "She did?" he asked.

"Yeah," said Maggie. "She really likes you, Dad."

"Hmmm," Jack said, releasing the little cat into Maggie's outstretched hands. He kissed his daughter's head and, at her insistence, kissed Bob's wet, anchovy-salty nose. "You think so?" he murmured, then turned off the light.

"Mmm," Maggie said.

He stroked her hair. It was fine and warm and slightly damp. "Maggie," he said softly, "she told you she likes me?"

"I could tell, Daddy," she said. " 'Night."

" 'Night," Jack said, pulling the comforter up over

her shoulders, then smoothing it idly, then drumming his fingers on it. "So did she say anything else?"

The couch creaked as Maggie turned over. "I don't know. I'm pretty tired, Daddy." She yawned vigorously. Then, her voice trailing off, she added, "I'm going to get to sleep now."

Jack rubbed his scalp. It was tender, but he hadn't broken the skin. "Er, Maggie," he called, shaking his head now, not believing he was going to say it: "So what are we going to do about those fish?"

"What?" she said.

He turned the light back on, then clapped his hands together. "We need to go buy new fish."

"Now?" she asked, blinking up at him.

He picked her up and hugged her and swung her around. "Sammy can't show up at school without the fish," he pointed out. "Mrs. Fineman will kill him." He set her down. "Here, put on your coat."

"But, Dad, I'm wearing pajamas."

"I know, Maggie-Mags, but—" He helped her into her little purple rain jacket and knelt down to snap shut the buckles. "We've got to help the poor kid out," he explained.

The fireworks extravaganza was in its booming, popping, fizzing finale as Jack and Maggie emerged from the building. He swept her up into his arms, where she watched the last embers of color drizzle from the night sky as he loped along toward Broadway.

"Where are we going to get fish, Daddy?" she asked, returning her attention to practical matters.

"This is New York, New York, Miss Magpie. The city that never sleeps. So nice they named it twice—"

"Yeah, but it's late, Dad—"

"Yeah, but we're on the West Side, Mags. If Fairway and Shakespeare & Company, and Barnes & Noble are open, so is the Pet Shed," he announced optimistically. "That's what I love about the West Side. You can pick up focaccio, arugula, a book, or a goldfish any time you please."

If you're well-coordinated enough, Jack silently amended five minutes later. He was plundering the Pet Shed's large, brightly lit tank, trying desperately to lure a fish into his tiny net. Maggie stood sleepily beside him. "Tell me again," Jack urged her. "What am I looking for?"

She yawned. "A gold one with like big wings, a skinny black one, and a red-and-white one with a mean face."

Exasperated, Jack tossed down the net and stuck his hands into the tank.

"Oh, Dad," Maggie said, rolling her eyes at him. "Oh, boy."

— **Fifteen** —

She was still in her suit skirt and silk blouse, plodding shoeless between the microwave and the sink, when the fireworks ended. "That was great, Mom. Wasn't it?" Sammy asked, entering the kitchen in his Gargoyle pajamas. "How come you didn't watch the whole thing?"

"You've got a milk mustache, sweetie," Mel said, scraping the peanut buttery bread crusts, the sticky peach pit, and the crumpled apple juice container from his Mighty Morphins lunch box into the garbage can. They tumbled in a succession of gooey plops onto the nested remains of Sammy's spaghetti dinner.

"Are you mad at me?"

Mel set down the lunch box and pulled a paper towel from the roll over the sink. "Of course not," she said, wiping the milk off his upper lip. "Why? Am I acting like I'm angry?"

Sammy shrugged. "Just like you're . . . I don't know, like sad maybe."

"Did you brush your teeth?" Mel asked. "I'm just tired, honey. It's been a really crazy day."

"Yeah," said Sammy, as the microwave beeped. "It was really, really crazy. I had a whole lot of fun, Mom."

Mel hurried to the microwave, stepping into a milk spill in front of the fridge. "Are you ready for bed, sweetie?" she asked, hopping, blotting the milk off the bottom of her stocking with the wadded paper towel. I'll be right in. Just brush, okay?"

"Can I watch a video before I go to sleep?"

"We'll see."

"You always say that," he grumbled, heading for the bathroom as she pulled the steaming pouch of vegetarian chop suey out of the micro. "And I don't want to see that stupid 'Snow White' one again with that stupid scary witch!"

"Fine—" Mel said, tossing the steaming pouch onto the counter, where it burst open, splashing her silk blouse and dribbling down onto her skirt. "Oh, no! Oh, God," she ranted, clumping toward the paper towels "Will this day ever end?"

The doorbell rang like a response from God. Wiping viscous veggies off her shirt, she stomped down the hall and opened the front door.

"Hi," Jack Taylor said, with his alluring, boyish grin.

"Hi," said Mel, dumbfounded, picking a bean sprout off her blouse.

He handed her a paper carton which looked suspiciously like a Chinese food container. The cuff of his extended sleeve was soaking wet. Impulsively, Mel blotted it with the chop suey wipe-up towel. Then, reddening, stepped back.

"Er, Maggie insisted we bring Sammy new fish," Jack said, gesturing to his daughter who, in bedroom slippers, pajamas, and her little purple raincoat, stood sleepily at his side.

"Well, thank you," Mel said, smiling at last. "You guys want to come in for a second?"

"Oh, no. We don't want to intrude," he insisted. "Do we?" he cued Maggie.

"Oh, please, Daddy," she said, and yawned again.

"Come on in. Really." Mel laughed.

"Well," he acquiesced. "Alright. Just for a few minutes."

Sammy padded out of his room. "Wow, Jack. Hi!" he enthused, adding a quieter, "Oh, hi," to Maggie.

Mel led them into the kitchen, mopping up the chop suey spill on the counter in passing. While she transferred the fish from the paper carton to a glass bowl of water, Jack inspected the apartment. He took in the opened garbage can, scattered toys, dishes in the sink, rain-soaked clothes flung over a chair.

Mel noticed him nodding. "You're investigating my apartment?" she asked.

"It's not as neat as I would have thought," he said, apparently pleased.

"It's only neat on Sunday mornings when my mother comes for brunch," she said, looking around for a safe place to store the fish. "If she sees it like this," she added, carrying the bowl across the kitchen and setting it down on the place mats on top of the refrigerator, "she shakes her head, which means she's unhappy with my life choices. Then she lets out a sigh that means she'd have rather gone to my sister's for brunch."

"I like Rita," Jack said.

"Mom, what about the video?" Sammy wanted to know.

"You guys want to watch a video?" Mel asked.

They nodded in unison, and when she said, "What about 'Mary Poppins'?" they both shouted, "Yeah!"

Mel took Maggie's hand and they followed Sammy into her bedroom. Searching among the cassettes on her dresser, she found "Mary Poppins" wedged between "Power Rangers" and "Gone With the Wind." There was a chocolate thumb print across Julie Andrews' face. "You can get all snuggled up in my bed and watch for a little while."

"I want to watch the whole thing, Mommy," Sammy insisted.

"It's too late. You can watch for as long as it takes us to drink one cup of coffee."

"Two," Sammy negotiated.

"We'll see," Mel said. She turned on the VCR, adjusted the sound and left them. Jack had wandered into the living room. He was studying the framed photographs on her bookshelf. They were mostly of Mel and Sammy, or just Sammy at various stages of his young life. There was also an oval framed portrait of her father as a young man, and one of the entire family, taken when she was eleven and used that year as a Christmas card.

"It's always such a dilemma when you've got kids." Jack set down the picture of Sammy drooling in ecstatic toothlessness. "I mean," he said, turning to Mel, "do you put out a picture of your ex so your kid feels like you're accepting and supportive of the other parent, or are you honest and say, 'I love *you*, kid, but I really can't stand to look at your mother's face anymore'?"

She laughed. "Right after Sammy's dad and I got divorced, I stuck pictures of him all over Sammy's room. I guess I was trying to reassure him that no matter what, his dad would still be in his life."

Jack nodded.

"Be right back," Mel said. She hurried into the kitchen and poured two cups of coffee for them, then threw open the cabinet above the sink and found the Pepperidge Farm cookies behind the Triscuits. She dumped the cookies onto a plate, removing three broken bits and quickly eating one of them.

"Sammy seems real proud of his dad," Jack said,

when she returned to the living room. She pushed a set of floor plans off the coffee table with her foot, then set down the tray. "He talked about him a lot today."

"I'm sure he did," she said with a hint of exasperation that was lost on Jack.

She handed him a mug of coffee. He took a sip, then said, "Is he really a rock-and-roll drummer?"

Mel grabbed a cookie, then leaned back on the couch. It felt unbelievably good to sit down. She propped her feet up on the coffee table and stretched languorously. "He's touring with Springsteen this summer."

"Really?" Jack was impressed. "Wow, Springsteen."

"Yeah," Mel said, studying the buttery little ring of shortbread, turning it in her hands as if seeking the perfect point of entry.

Jack smiled, uncomfortable suddenly. He began to tap his fingers on the mug. Finally, he cleared his throat. "Look," he said, more aggressively than he'd meant to, "I've been beating around the bush long enough, I guess. There's something I've just got to ask you."

She smiled. "Yes?" she said.

"Why did you spend the whole day flirting with me if you're thinking of getting back together with your ex-husband?"

Her mouth fell open. "What?" she said with a frozen smile. "Excuse me, but I spent the whole day disliking you," she corrected him, tossing the cookie back onto the tray and wiping her hands free of crumbs. "Intensely," she added. "*You* were flirting with me. You even told the kids you wanted to ask me out . . . and here you are."

Jack put down his cup. "I never told them that," he said.

"Yes you did," Mel insisted. "It was your big secret. They told me it was all about you and me and going somewhere and feelings. You were going to ask me out."

"Big secret?" Jack said. "The only big secret was about Sammy putting my marble up his nose."

She narrowed her eyes at him. So he chuckled debonairly and said, "I never once thought about asking you out."

"Oh, I'm so sure," she said.

"Never once—"

She shook her head, dismissing his interruption. "You were checking me out on the street in front of the newspaper stand before we even got to the school this morning."

"Doesn't count," he said. "I didn't know that was you."

She burst out laughing. "But then when you found out it was me, you shoved your column in my face because you thought I was the most beautiful woman you'd ever seen."

He grinned. "You believed that line?"

She dropped her feet to the floor and sat up. "That

was not a line, Jack, and you know it. You've wanted me," she continued, adjusting her position on the couch, folding her legs under her and turning to face him, "ever since I knew you were a writer because you said *your* attitude was derived from *my* attitude."

His grin was widening. It wasn't his winning grin either, he knew. It wasn't The Smile. It was goony, childlike, irrepressible, the kind of grin that mocks your determination to be serious and self-righteous. "And you've wanted me," he argued, "ever since the Ninety-eighth Street Day Care Center when you saw me saying goodbye to Maggie but you didn't know it was me."

"Hah!" She shifted, leaned closer to him, and stuck out her chin. "For someone who is so totally uninterested in the other person, you sure do remember every single minute detail of this entire day."

He set down his cup. "You remember it better than I do," he said.

She flounced beside him. "I do not."

"Yes you do," he asserted, mimicking the antagonistic set of her jaw—although her gaze was full of laughter, eyes crinkling smartly at the corners.

"No I don't," she insisted, pushing her face still closer to his.

Her soft, warm breath brushed his lips like a Carribean breeze. "What would you do if I kissed you right now?" he asked. He'd wanted to make a joke of it, to pretend he was just taunting her, but his voice broke mid-sentence and he sounded like an adolescent geek.

He didn't care.

"You're not going to kiss me right now," she challenged in an amused whisper.

"Do you *want* me to kiss you right now?" Jack asked. He could barely get his eyes to focus. She was too near and too warm. Her face was a pale velvety blur around those slightly smiling, amazingly full lips.

She chuckled, a cute, throaty little sound, like a pigeon cooing. She said, "Do *you* want to kiss me right now?"

Jack stood up suddenly and, looking down at her, cleared his throat. "I wouldn't have mentioned it if I didn't," he announced.

"Fine," she said.

"You're just reeling me in, aren't you?" he asked, offering her his hands. She was grinning up at him, but he wasn't smiling now. It wasn't that he didn't want to; it just wasn't happening. She let him help her to her feet. "Like Roy Scheider at the end of 'Jaws,'" he heard himself saying. They were wedged into the narrow trench between the coffee table and the sofa. "The minute I open my mouth, you're going to throw a big bomb in it," he murmured, his lips very close to hers. "Then you'll wear my teeth around your neck."

"So," she whispered, "you're admitting you're a big shark?"

"I'm admitting," he said, softly, seriously, before

he could stop himself, "that I'm terrified of getting close to anyone again."

"I'm just as scared as you are," Mel said quickly.

He believed her. And anyway, those wonderful lips were so close, so ready. "Don't bite," he whispered.

"I won't," she promised, closing her eyes.

"Mommy? Mom?"

Mel's eyes snapped open. Jack's head whipped toward the doorway. Looking desperate and small in his Gargoyle pj's, Sammy said, "Can you fast forward for us? That bird lady is on and we hate that part."

"Sammy, you know how to fast forward," Mel said, turning toward him.

"Uh-uh," he replied, shaking his head. "The remote isn't working. And, Mommy, you know, Mom, that lady is so creepy."

"Alright," she said. "Go back in and I'll be right there."

Obediently, Sammy hiked up his droopy pajama bottoms and shuffled back to his mother's room. Mel looked at Jack. "Right," he said, stepping toward her again.

"No, wait. Let's do this right," she said, touching his cheek thoughtfully, then surveying her chop suey–soiled blouse, her short skirt twisted almost backwards now, stained and wrinkled. "Let me go freshen up so I feel a little more like a woman instead of a dead mommy." She nudged him gently back onto the couch. "You sit here, close your eyes, lay your head back, and anticipate my return. Or else just watch 'Mary Poppins' until I get back."

"I'll be here," he decided.

After fast forwarding the video for Maggie and Sammy, Mel fast forwarded herself into the bathroom and embarked on a speed overhaul. The most important thing, she told herself, as she washed her face, brushed her teeth, swished mouthwash around her gums, and picked up the hairbrush for a quick follicle training session, was to focus on the chores directly in front of her and not on the big, handsome, irresistibly adorable man waiting in the next room. Because if she did that, she thought, removing her food-splattered silk blouse and exchanging it for the tiny T-shirt hanging to dry in the shower, if she focused on Jack, thought for even a minute about what she might be getting herself into . . .

She threw open the laundry hamper and foraged for the pair of not too dirty jeans she'd tossed in the night before. If she tried to get rational about well, really, what little she knew about this guy whom she'd met less than twenty-four hours ago and had totally hated because of his casual parenting, over-inflated ego, and pretentious boasting . . .

What was worse, Mel realized at the same moment that she noticed her legs needed shaving, was that he knew practically nothing about her. And when he found out, she thought, throwing a leg onto the sink and lathering up, when he discovered who *she* really was . . . pushy, perfectionistic, demanding . . . And all of it a front for . . . what? Feeling scared and dismally inadequate as a parent, feeling less like a mother than the designated bailer in a two-person rowboat on a constantly storm-tossed sea . . .

Mel grabbed the razor and nicked herself just below the knee as the realization washed over her that she was nothing special and that this was hopeless and that there was no reason a funny, bright, good-looking guy like Jack would be attracted to someone as alternately arrogant and helpless as she . . .

Like a shark, like Jaws, the critic had smelled blood and was back with a vengeance. Wincing, Mel wet a piece of toilet tissue and stemmed the shallow bleeding on her shin. As she rinsed her razor, she had a vision of Jack as Roy Scheider, Robert Shaw, and Richard Dreyfuss all rolled into one. And she could practically feel his hand on hers as she turned on the water full force and drowned the damned critic once and for all.

She shimmied into her jeans, slathered body lotion on her exposed parts—arms, hands, neck, feet— clipped a broken toenail, and spritzed herself with the Body Shop's new spring scent, which was as redolent with hope as a rain-soaked garden. Then twirling in front of the full-length mirror attached to the bathroom door, she saw, with rare satisfaction, that she looked casual, clean, and, yes, even sexy.

"Everything okay?" she asked the kids on her way through the bedroom. Sammy gave her a happy thumbs-up sign in passing; Maggie's heavy-lidded eyes were glued to Dick Van Dyke.

In the living room, Jack was resting on the sofa with his eyes closed and his head laid back against a cushion. Melanie came around the couch and sat down next to him.

He didn't move.

She made a little noise and settled herself closer. Still, he didn't stir. She moved her face very close to his. She could smell his aftershave and the earthy wet scent of his hair. She watched his closed eyelids, his dark, long lashes resting motionless against the bluish hollows under his eyes. Saw his lips, slightly parted, and the glint of his handsome teeth. She moved closer, watching him, waiting. And he snored. There was nothing subtle about it. It was a big, window-rattling, freight train of a snore. He was fast asleep.

Mel sighed, then leaned back against the sofa and stared at the ceiling, which she'd painted a restful eggshell blue. Aside from a small section near the steampipe where a piece of plaster had cracked off, it was pure and peaceful. Aside from the faint, carefree music, so familiar that she could picture Julie Andrews and Dick Van Dyke gamboling among the penguins, and the distant giggles of two little kids up way past their bedtime, the apartment was placid, still.

Mel allowed her eyes to close. She felt her head loll gently as she sank into the comfortable sofa cushions.

Before she drifted off to sleep, she noticed three things: that there was nothing she needed to remember for tomorrow—no list to make, no perils to avert, no precautions to take; that the demanding demon in her head was silent and had remained so for nearly fifteen minutes, ever since Jack had helped her drown it in the bathroom sink; and that Jack's arm had somehow circled her shoulder and her cheek had somehow found his chest, and that they were breathing so flawlessly together it was impossible to tell where one left off and the other began.

Against the backdrop of an elegant Cornwall man-
sion before World War II and a vast continent-
spanning canvas during the turbulent war years,
Rosamunde Pilcher's most eagerly-awaited novel is
the story of an extraordinary young woman's coming of age, coming to grips with love and sadness,
and in every sense of the term, coming home...

Rosamunde Pilcher

The #1 *New York Times* Bestselling Author of *The Shell Seekers* and *September*

COMING HOME

"Rosamunde Pilcher's most satisfying story since *The Shell Seekers*."

—*Chicago Tribune*

"Captivating...The best sort of book to come home
to...Readers will undoubtedly hope Pilcher comes home
to the typewriter again soon."

—*New York Daily News*

COMING HOME
Rosamunde Pilcher
_____ 95812-9 $7.99 U.S./$9.99 CAN.

Publishers Book and Audio Mailing Service
P.O. Box 070059, Staten Island, NY 10307
Please send me the book(s) I have checked above. I am enclosing $_____ (please add
$1.50 for the first book, and $.50 for each additional book to cover postage and handling.
Send check or money order only—no CODs) or charge my VISA, MASTERCARD,
DISCOVER or AMERICAN EXPRESS card.

Card Number_____

Expiration date_____Signature_____

Name_____

Address_____

City_____State/Zip _____
Please allow six weeks for delivery. Prices subject to change without notice. Payment in
U.S. funds only. New York residents add applicable sales tax.   CH 8/96

Two Italian immigrant brothers, Primo and Secondo, have come to a small seaside town in New Jersey in search of the American dream. Primo is an artist in the kitchen, truly ahead of his time, while Secondo is the front man, doing his best to make their restaurant a success.

But business is bad at The Paradise. Confused by Primo's culinary creations, customers flock instead to Pascal's, the rival restaurant across the street that serves up bad food and tacky decor. And now Secondo has learned that the bank is about to foreclose.

When the unpredictable Pascal proposes that the brothers host a dinner party for jazz great Louis Prima, Secondo jumps at the chance. But will the glorious feast the brothers cook up make their reputation and save their dream? And will their relationship survive the big night?

Big Night
Joseph Tropiano

BASED ON THE SCREENPLAY BY STANLEY TUCCI AND JOSEPH TROPIANO

NOW A MAJOR MOTION PICTURE STARRING MINNIE DRIVER, IAN HOLM, ISABELLA ROSSELLINI, TONY SHALHOUB, AND STANLEY TUCCI

A ST. MARTIN'S GRIFFIN TRADE PAPERBACK

BIG NIGHT
Joseph Tropiano
_____ 14844-5 $9.95 U.S./$13.99 CAN.

Publishers Book and Audio Mailing Service
P.O. Box 070059, Staten Island, NY 10307
Please send me the book(s) I have checked above. I am enclosing $_____ (please add $3.00 for the first book, and $.50 for each additional book to cover postage and handling. Send check or money order only—no CODs) or charge my VISA, MASTERCARD, DISCOVER or AMERICAN EXPRESS card.

Card Number_____

Expiration date_____Signature_____

Name_____

Address_____

City_____State/Zip _____
Please allow six weeks for delivery. Prices subject to change without notice. Payment in U.S. funds only. New York residents add applicable sales tax.   BN 1/97